I0625071

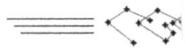

An injured veterinarian and a cyborg with unusual pets must join forces to save their town.

The vast Central Galactic Concordance strictly prohibits genetic experimentation and alteration of humans on any of its 500 member planets. Animals aren't so lucky.

On a frontier planet, veterinarian **Bethnee Bakonin** made a home for herself in the frozen north. Her minder talent for healing all kinds of animals would ordinarily assure her success, but her unwilling stint in the shady pet trade industry left her damaged and scared. She works around her limitations as best she can, and rescues pet trade castoffs.

"Volunteered" for a black-box research project, elite forces Jumper **Axur Tragon** now has dangerous experimental tech in his cybernetic limbs. He escaped and crash-landed a stolen freighter in the northern mountains of a frontier planet, only to discover a secret shipment of designer pets was part of the cargo. Determined to do right by them, he enlists reluctant Bethnee's aid in caring for them—a definite challenge, considering Bethnee is terrified of him.

When greedy mercenaries come raiding, can Axur and Bethnee work together to overcome their limitations, with help from their unusual pets, and save the day?

ALSO BY CAROL VAN NATTA

Central Galactic Concordance Space Opera Series

- Last Ship Off Polaris-G (Novella)
- Overload Flux (Book 1)
- Minder Rising (Book 2)
- Zero Flux (Novella)
- Pico's Crush (Book 3)
- Pet Trade (Novella)
- Jumper's Hope (Book 4)
- Cats of War (Novella)
- Galactic Search and Rescue (Novella)
- Escape from Nova Nine (Novella)
- Spark Transform (Book 5)

Paranormal Romance

- Shifter Mate Magic (Ice Age Shifters #1)
- Shift of Destiny (Ice Age Shifters #2)
- Heart of a Dire Wolf (Ice Age Shifters #3)
- Dire Wolf Wanted (Ice Age Shifters #4)
- Shifter's Storm (Ice Age Shifters #5)
- In Graves Below (Magic, NM)

Retro Science Fiction Comedy

- Hooray for Holopticon

PET TRADE

A CENTRAL GALACTIC CONCORDANCE
NOVELLA

CAROL VAN NATTA

Location: Frontier Planet Del'Arche * GDAT 3241.155

Veterinary medic Bethnee Bakonin limped toward the cage slowly. The huge dire wolf inside stood and eyed her with wary interest, but not fear or anger. The wolf's bright blue, intelligent eyes contrasted beautifully against her thick coat of charcoal grey and black fur. Bethnee reached out with another thread of her talent to get a sense of the designer animal's health. "Where did she come from?"

A capricious, chilly wind blew a dust devil into the

center of the paddock, then let it go. Fall always arrived early in the foothills of the northernmost mountains on Del'Arche.

"A boutique alpaca ranch down south. New client." Nuñez frowned and crossed her arms. "Idiots thought a top-of-the-line, protector-class dire wolf would make a great herd dog." She made a disgusted sound. "They were going to shoot her because she wouldn't let the herd out of the barn. I convinced them to sign her over to me."

Bethnee eyed Nuñez. "How much did she cost?" Designer animals from reputable pet-trade dealers weren't cheap. Recreating extinct mammals from Earth's Pleistocene period was perennially popular, because it avoided the Central Galactic Concordance government's multiple prohibitions against altering cornerstone species like wolves and coyotes. Bethnee had been saving her hard credits to buy her own flitter, instead of constantly having to borrow Nuñez's, but the rescued dire wolf took priority.

Nuñez shook her head. "Zero. They bought her cheap with a flatlined ID chip, so she's probably stolen. I told them I'd take care of the problem for free, and that it'd be our little secret." Knowing Nuñez, she'd pushed them with her low-level empath talent, so they'd be afraid of getting caught, and happy to be rid of the evidence. Nuñez had no compunction against using her minder talent to manipulate humans who hurt animals, which was one of several reasons why she and Bethnee got along so well.

Bethnee focused on sensing the wolf's mind. The fleeting thoughts were complex, with deep memories. The wolf had known and felt pack love for other humans, but hadn't seen them for a long time. The ranchers had beaten her to get her into the cage, and she didn't know what she'd done wrong.

Bethnee contained her talent and her anger, then told Nuñez what she'd found. "She's also got tracers in every major joint. Can I use your small surgical suite this afternoon?" The portable unit contained micro surgical tools with an AI-assist built in, and would make quick work of the excisions.

"Sure." Nuñez tilted her head toward the doors of the vetmed clinic behind her. "Let's get her inside."

"Does she respond to a name?"

"Didn't come up." Nuñez looked at the clock. "I'll make you a deal. After I put the flitter away, you help me feed and water the yaks, and I'll help you with the tracers."

"It'll snow tonight." Nuñez lifted the last bulky bag of feed and unsealed it. At age one hundred and nine, the woman looked like a plump rural grandmother who printed heritage quilts and baked cookies, but she was strong and smart, and could control a herd of fifty large buffalo with her minder talent.

Bethnee took the bag. "The weather AI doesn't think so." She angled her hip so she didn't stress her bad leg, then reached high to pour the bag's contents into the hopper.

"The yaks say otherwise." Nuñez took the empty bag. "They're huddling in the corner of the pen near the barn.

Weather AI says it'll be a bad winter." She gave Bethnee a meaningful look. "You could move back to the clinic."

"We've been..." Bethnee began, then sighed. "I'm fine where I am. It suits me."

Nuñez continued as if she hadn't heard. "Still plenty of room in the clinic. You could live next door, because that hateful Raloff family abandoned the property to move deeper into the mountains." She headed for the sink to wash her hands. "If we shared the clinic again, you could actually leave town for more than a few hours and know your animals were safe, and maybe have your leg fixed. You're too young to be a hermit. You're homesteaded now, and the town would be happy to have you."

"No, they wouldn't." Bethnee followed Nuñez to the sink. "Too many people considered my animals a nuisance." She pointed her chin toward the big cage. "The first goat or child that went missing, they'd accuse the dire wolf. Or Jynx." Unusual snow leopards, no matter how well behaved, scared people who didn't know them.

As Bethnee washed her hands, Nuñez turned on the mini-solardry. "It was only the Raloffs and Administrator Pranteaux who complained, and he complains about everything." They both rubbed their hands vigorously in the warm, forced air. "Come on. Let's take care of your new wolf."

Bethnee was grateful that her friend hadn't gotten into the real reasons Bethnee couldn't move back. A lot of frontier settlers like the Raloffs had moved away from the Central Galactic Concordance member planets to get away from minders, and everyone knew she was one, because she used her talents as well as her training to treat pets. Word got around.

More importantly, even though she'd escaped her former life in the pet trade three years ago, she still couldn't get within five meters of any man without taking the chance she'd be shaking like a leaf from mind-numbing fear. When she'd first arrived, she couldn't even be in the same building. She'd gotten better with time, but it was bad for business when she couldn't deal with nearly half the population of customers.

Nuñez claimed it was post-trauma stress, and just like her leg, it could be treated by competent medics and minders. Even if that were true, it would cost hard credit, and she needed every decimal she had to provide for her animal family. They didn't care that she was too scared and too damaged to live among humans.

2

* GDAT 3241.155 *

Axur Tragon fought the rising wind to land the old runabout as gently as he could on the Tanimai community airpad. He retracted the canopy and climbed out, then stepped around back to open the hatch and untie the two covered carriers. "Almost there," he crooned.

He slung the straps on each of his shoulders, then walked to Tanimai's vetmed clinic. His cybernetic legs weren't pretty, but they gave him a long, smooth gait, even when carrying a thirty-kilo load.

He'd only been in town a dozen times since he'd landed three hundred local days ago on the frontier planet of Del'Arche. Crashed, really, but his former Jumper Corps flight instructor said as long as the pilot and passengers crawled away, it counted as a landing.

He hoped the veterinary medic wouldn't turn him away. Between his intimidating height, his long, shaggy hair, and his bizarre and heavy metallic poncho, he looked like a disaster refugee with mental issues. Throw in the scars and the visible cybernetics, and he probably scared birds from the sky.

The shallow lobby was open, but deserted. He stepped up to the wallcomp. "Hello?"

An older woman's face appeared on the display. "Be there in a minute. Set the carriers on the table."

He complied, after first testing the table to make sure it would hold.

Moments later, the interior sliding doors opened and revealed the woman he'd spoken to. She had black hair streaked with silver, and a pleasant smile. "I'm Aniashalaman Nuñez, the VMD. Call me Nuñez." She looked up at him from her considerably shorter height. "You must be the ex-Jumper, Axur Tragon. You're as tall as everyone says." Despite her Islander complexion and facial features, her accent was pure Standard English.

He returned her smile. "I'm actually short, for a Jumper."

Nuñez laughed and shaded her eyes as she looked up. "From down here, you all look like trees to me." She tilted her head toward the table. "What can I help you with?"

"I have some, uh, pets, and these are sick, I think." He shoved his hands in his pockets under his heavy poncho. "To be honest, I kind of inherited them, and don't know much about their care, except what I read in reference manuals. They all did okay in the spring and summer, but lately, these aren't."

"How many pets do you have?" Nuñez crossed to the table and lifted the cover on the first cage. "Ah, birds of paradise. Three females and a male. Are they mated?"

"No clue. To answer your first question, seven if you count species, and twelve animals total. I think they're all designer, rather than domestic." He tilted his head toward the second cage. "I don't even know what some of them are."

Nuñez lifted the cover of the second carrier. "Great balls of chaos, what a..." Nuñez pulled the cover off completely. "...chimera."

Axur suspected she'd censored a less diplomatic description. He couldn't blame her. Kivo was German shepherd-sized, but the resemblance ended there. He had black and brown stripes in his short, sleek fur, and six legs with clawed paws for running and catching. Gigantic, bat-style swivel ears sat on his broad, flat head. He had two tails with tufts of black fur on the ends. He was a prime example of what the anti-pet-trade activists railed against: tinkering with Terran genetics to create whimsical animals that would have never survived in the wild, much less natural selection. Kivo might be a genetic mess, but he was also the sweetest, most laid-back beast Axur had ever met, and was patient with all the animals, even the miniature dinosaur that often mistook Kivo's tails as something edible. "Kivo's usually interested in everything, and eats anything, but not for the past week. The birds just huddle in the bottom of their cage and won't go out."

Nuñez made a face. "I might be able to help with the birds, but Kivo is about as far off my chart as you can get. My patients are large herd animals and the occasional terrier or tabby. You need a specialist." She glanced up at him and sighed. "As it happens, I know one of the best in the galaxy, but she's not..."

A cacophony of goose honking from somewhere in the building interrupted. Nuñez glanced toward the back and frowned. "Sit a minute." She pointed to a lobby chair, then strode through the doors she'd come through and vanished. The doors slid quickly closed behind her.

He dragged the chair closer to the table and sat, putting his face closer to Kivo's cage. The chimera rolled back in the cage and exposed his striped stomach. "Sorry, buddy, no belly rubs until they give me permission to let you out."

Axur looked up when the clinic's outside doors opened to admit a tall, willowy woman with shoulder-length, deep blue-black hair and Asian features. She carried several bags and a box, and walked with a pronounced limp. She glanced at him, startled. "Does Nuñez know..." She trailed off as her attention riveted on Kivo.

After a long moment, Axur answered her unfinished question. "Nuñez asked me to wait here."

She darted a look to his face and awkwardly backed up several steps, dropping one of the bags. "Oh."

He started to stand and reach out to help her, but froze in mid-rise when her eyes widened in unmistakable fear. Her hand visibly trembled as she awkwardly scooped up the bag, then fled through the doors to the back.

He sat down again with a sigh. It never paid to play the shoulda-coulda-woulda game, but starting a year ago, it was hard not to wish for a different star lane for his life. He'd never been nova-hot beautiful like some in his squad, but he'd never lacked for companionship and bed partners for his twelve years in the CPS Jumper Corps. Then, unbeknownst to him, he'd been secretly selected for a CPS "special project" that changed him forever, including adding valuable experimental tech to his cybernetics.

Now he was an ugly mass of biometal and hardware that made him a walking, talking satellite uplink. Only the heavy poncho he'd kludged together from salvaged supplies kept him from constantly broadcasting his unique comm signature to the frontier planet's various satellites, and from there to the Central Galactic Concordance's intergalactic communications network. If he uncloaked, his days of freedom remaining would be measured by how fast a CPS ship could get to Del'Arche to hunt him down.

Kivo whined. Axur stuck his fingers into the cage again and tried to shake off his melancholy. He'd lived, and so had Kivo and the others, and life was hope.

Ten minutes later, Nuñez strode back into the lobby, looking harried. "Thanks for waiting." She put her fists on her hips. "I have an emergency, so I'll cut to the chase. I can't treat your pets, but Bethnee Bakonin can. She's the woman who just came in. She's already seen you, and that's usually a deal-killer for her, but if you keep your distance and don't make sudden movements, she'll look at your animals." Her chin jutted out pugnaciously. "She's a pet-trade expert, but she's also a pan-phyla animal-affinity talent, so if you dislike minders, you can jet right now, 'cause I'm one, too."

Axur put his hands flat on his thighs. "Minders are just people. I don't care if she uses dark energy magic, if she can help Kivo and the birds." He pointed a thumb toward the front doors. "I could wait outside."

Nuñez shook her head. "No, she'll need information from you. Just move your chair away and stay seated." She glanced at his stained pants and worn combat boots. "I'll assume you're not offering hard credit. What are you trading?"

"Fall harvest gourds, berries, and leafy greens. If it's more than that, we can negotiate." In the planet's official financial transaction records, the town's economy was barely a blip, but it did a thriving business in trade. From what he'd gathered, the settlement company took a percentage of all financial transactions, but hadn't found a way to close the trading loophole, so they often conducted unannounced audits, trying to catch the town breaking the rules so they could levy hard-credit fines. They took a percentage of those transactions, too.

Nuñez nodded. "Fair enough." She gave him a considering look. "Bakonin is like most high-level animal-affinity talents, better with animals than people, and like a lot of us here in Tanimai,"—she looked pointedly at the visible scars on his neck and jaw leading up to his disabled skulljack—"she's had a hard life. Be respectful, and she'll do right by you and the animals. Scare her, and you'll never see her again."

Axur didn't miss the unspoken warning that he'd never trade in town again if he did anything to make Bakonin bolt. "Understood."

He carried the chair to the far corner and sat, then hunched over to rest his elbows on his knees. It was as short as he could make himself.

Nuñez left. The doors stayed open long enough for Bakonin to limp in. She glanced at him briefly as she made her way to the table. Her shuttered expression changed to interest when she got to the birds.

Axur watched as she opened the cage with the four birds and deftly pulled the brightly colored male out and turned him upside down to look at his chest and feet. "Yes, yes," she said soothingly. Her voice had a warm, husky timbre. She did the same with the others, then closed the cage door.

She took a deep breath, let it out slowly, then turned to look at him. "Nuñez said you've only had the animals for about nine months, and that you've got more at home. Were they in your ship when you crashed?"

Axur looked up at her, startled. "How did you know about the ship?"

One corner of her mouth twitched. "Hard to miss a streaking fireball that left a kilometer-long gouge at the north end of Park Plateau. No one knew anyone had survived until you came into town two weeks later offering exotic trade goods. People talk." She pointed skyward. "You're lucky the weather satellites were malfing again, or the company auditors would have levied a huge fine for terraform destruction, confiscated anything you had of value, then expatriated you to the nearest Concordance lockup for illegal trespass and occupation."

He ducked his head, embarrassed that it hadn't occurred to him that others might have seen his ungraceful entry into Del'Arche's atmosphere. "I didn't know about the animals until the hard landing ripped open the freighter's smuggling hold. I've tried to care for those that lived. The ship's library has good reference files."

Bakonin nodded. "Pet-trade dealers often ship on the sly to get around inspections and quarantines, and to deter thieves. It's a ruthless business." She pointed to the cage. "Your birds are healthy, but cold intolerant. If you don't give them a warm habitat and a diet of insects and fruit, they'll die. They're fertile, so if you do have a habitat, you'll have fledglings by the spring."

"Okay." He could work around the diet problem, but had no idea how he'd create a warm space out of the ship's wreckage, miscellaneous cargo, and the deadfall trees he'd hauled in for building materials. The possibility of offspring hadn't even crossed his mind. Like everyone else in the Concordance, he'd gotten a birth control implant at the first hint of puberty, so reproduction took a deliberate decision between two people.

She turned to the chimera. Kivo exhibited intense curiosity, his leaf-shaped nose working and his ears swiveling forward. He stood, briefly, but his two back sets of legs shook, and he half sat. She opened the cage door. Kivo oozed out and crouched. She approached slowly, then gently ran her hands over his ribs, shoulder joints, and sharply articulated spine. Kivo leaned into her as she crooned nonsense words while she examined his ears, eyes, and wicked-looking teeth. He was soon rolling onto his back, stretching his six legs out, begging for attention. She smiled and rubbed his belly, and even laughed when he sloppily licked her nose when she got close enough. "Does he have a name?"

Axur was so mesmerized by her obvious skill and the glimpse of beauty in her smile that it took him a moment to realize she was talking to him. "Kivo."

She kept one hand on Kivo's broad head and stroked his ear muscles with her thumb. "I'm guessing you fed him fresh meat and produce from your garden, which is the best thing you could have done, because it's kept him alive. The dealer was probably returning him to the research company's designers as a failure." Sadness stole across her face. "Even if we eradicate the blood parasite and tailor some nutritional chems to counter the anemia it caused, which is his current issue, other problems are coming. He's already got early-onset arthritis, especially in his double hips and flexible spine, and his fine-motor control is degrading."

It sounded like Kivo had the chimera equivalent of waster's disease, a pernicious problem that plagued Jumper veterans across the galaxy. The CPS researchers conducting the "special project" claimed to have cured him of it as compensation for taking his arm. Last he'd heard, that was impossible, so he really hoped that wasn't another one of their lies. His tried not to focus on his resentment and turned his attention back to Kivo. "Why did they create him at all?"

She shrugged. "Pretend alien fauna for the wealthy, maybe? It's a fad." She stroked the large hump of Kivo's middle shoulder joints. "The bio-engineers actually got the six legs to work, but the rest of him is a fantasy hodgepodge." She snorted disdainfully. "Two tails." She rested her hip against the table and eased the weight off her stiffer leg.

"He follows me everywhere. He keeps the peace among the other animals, too." He tilted his head. "Can animals be empaths? I think he tries to cheer me up sometimes." It sounded daft after he said it out loud, so he was grateful she didn't laugh.

"Maybe?" She shrugged. "Human medical scientists still don't know what combination of DNA and subtrans amino arrays make the difference between human minders and non-minders, or even predict the gender expression continuum. Who's to say that animals aren't evolving along with us?"

"Makes sense to me. What's the treatment protocol for him?"

"A tailored antibiotic to kill the parasite and immune boosters. If we can't trade with the local chems and alterants shop, we might have to use hard credit at the human med clinic down in Asgorth."

"I've got some reserve freighter stock to trade." He sat up straight and immediately regretted it, because it caused Bakonin to catch her breath and step back. "Sorry." He hunched over again.

Bakonin's lips thinned, and she shook her head. "I just hadn't realized how tall you are. Ex-Jumper?"

Axur gave her a humorless smile and held up his left hand, where exposed biometal gleamed at his knuckles. "My cybernetic arm and legs didn't give it away?" Most people preferred flesh and bone.

"Cybernetics are fine." She took a deep breath and let it out. "I'm phobic around men, sometimes, which is my problem, not yours."

Kivo's ears swiveled toward the sliding doors, and he rolled to a sitting position. A moment later, Nuñez appeared, the front of her tunic covered in blood. "I need your help."

3

After Bethnee hosed down the instruments of the large-animal surgical suite with steaming hot water, she stood next to the floor drain and turned the hose on her unlovely but waterproof, tear-resistant work tunic.

Axur, as he'd asked them to call him, had proven to be more than just a pretty face. Nuñez dragooned him into helping extricate a buffalo cow from a tangled coil of spikewire. Nuñez used her minder talent to control the cow while Axur used the superior strength of his cybernetic hand to stop the wire from springing out when Bethnee cut it. As long as she stayed on the other side of the cow and focused on using her talent to heal the cow's deepest lacerations, she'd managed to keep her mind clear and her stupid shaking to a minimum. Nevertheless, she felt like she'd hiked to the top of towering Mount Taruka and back.

Axur hadn't flinched at the blood or injuries. When

Nuñez commented on it, he'd admitted he'd been a trained field medic in the Jumper Corps.

Nuñez had laughed. "What the hell are you doing trying to make a homestead the hard way? The townspeople would be thrilled to build you a clinic, like they did mine."

Axur had looked away and mumbled something about it being complicated. Bethnee sympathized. She lived that every day.

Axur turned out to have another invaluable skill. The rattled, panicky owner of the cow only spoke halting English, but Axur figured out the woman spoke Korean, and served as their translator. He admitted to speaking eight languages fluently, and could get by in a lot more. Bethnee knew Nuñez was adding it to her arsenal of arguments of why he should move to town. Under her bluff and blunt exterior, Nuñez had a heart the size of the Andromeda galaxy, and didn't believe in complications.

It fell to Bethnee, with Axur's translation help, to negotiate a complex trade for their cow-saving services that resulted in Axur getting the drugs he needed for his chimera using a credit the rancher had at the chems shop, in exchange for Axur giving his food-trade goods to Nuñez, who would share them with Bethnee so she could make further trades for the ingredients for nutritional supplements for her animals and Kivo.

Bethnee found Nuñez and Axur in the holding pen outside. Unexpectedly, the chimera and the dire wolf also roamed the pen, pretending disinterest in one another. Bethnee sent a thread of her talent out to both animals, and found that Kivo considered the wolf a new friend, and the wolf was considering everyone in the pen, including Bethnee, as potential pack mates that needed guarding from the dangerous, grunting yaks in the neighboring paddock.

Axur laughed at something Nuñez said. Despite his untamed hair and the peculiar cloak he refused to remove, he was a surprisingly handsome man, especially when he smiled. And such was the irrational tangle of her phobia that she could admire a tall, good-natured man from afar, then be too scared to get close enough to see the color of his eyes.

"I'm going to remove the tracers from the wolf," she said loudly. "Want me to do the same for Kivo while I'm at it?"

Axur gave her a puzzled look. "Tracers?"

When Nuñez explained about the pet-trade practice of implanting active tracers that broadcast a valuable animal's location to the net, and passive tracers that showed up on bio scanners, Axur readily agreed.

With Nuñez's help and the portable surgical suite's micro instruments, Bethnee finished with both animals in thirty minutes. Nuñez planned to trade the active tracers to a client who could use them for tracking goats.

In the lobby, Kivo sidled up to the tolerant wolf and licked at her muzzle. Bethnee could well believe that Kivo was the peacekeeper among Axur's menagerie.

Nuñez entered and crossed to Axur to hand him a cup of hot coffee.

He smiled as he closed his eyes and smelled it, then sipped it with obvious enjoyment. "Stars, but I've missed this."

Nuñez grinned and sipped from her own cup. "I trade for it whenever I can." She pointed a thumb toward Bethnee. "Don't ever let Bethnee make it for you, unless you have a biometal stomach."

Bethnee shrugged. It tasted like burned acid to her, so how was she to know what was too strong? A thigh muscle in her bad leg spasmed. She needed to soak in her single luxury, the geothermal pool. She should just go home and...

"Dammit," she said. "I can't take the wolf with me today. I only have the glide board, and no den big enough for her." She caught Nuñez's eye. "Can she stay a few days?"

"Sure, but she'll be alone except for the geese and the yaks, and she'll hate it."

"I know you don't know me or my setup," said Axur, "but I could take her for as long as you need. My barn is big, and she wouldn't lack for company."

Bethnee looked at him in surprise.

Axur splayed his hands. "I have an ulterior motive. I was hoping you'd come out to my place and look at the rest of my pets. Tell me what they are, and how to care for them."

Nuñez nodded. "You can borrow the flitter."

The idea of going alone to a man's homestead spiked Bethnee's anxiety, but Axur had scrupulously accommodated her by keeping his distance, and it was a good solution for the new wolf. If she didn't like what she saw, she could jet. Besides, she had to admit she wanted to see the exotic animals Axur had told them about.

"Okay."

Axur looked pleased.

Nuñez blinked and raised her eyebrows. "You trust him?"

Bethnee pointed to the chimera, draped across Axur's sturdy cybernetic knees like a lapdog, and the wolf, who was licking Axur's hand.

"I trust them."

4

If Bethnee hadn't been following Axur's runabout, she wouldn't have found his high-country homestead. Which, she surmised, was as deliberate as his choice to stay away from town, as well as his choice to wear his awkward heavy cloak.

She landed the flitter in a clearing about a hundred meters southwest of the edge of his loosely fenced perimeter. She wished she'd thought to bring her glide board, to save her leg from the uphill hike while carrying her vetmed bag. Fortunately, the dire wolf stayed near with very little coaxing via her talent.

Axur backed up as she approached, staying well out of her discomfort range. "Sorry, I didn't think about the distance." Behind him rose two buildings fashioned out of starship freighter sections. The taller one had wide doors made from an airlock. "It's windy up here, so I want to give you an earwire so we can talk without shouting. It'll take me a few minutes to program."

"Okay." The wolf remained by her side, nose working overtime as she checked out her new surroundings. Bethnee reached out with her talent to do the same.

Axur cleared his throat. "Some of the animals are in the barn." He pointed toward wide, open doors. "I'll knock on the wall when I'm ready with the earwire."

FORTY MINUTES LATER, Bethnee sat on a rough-hewn bench at the worktable inside the barn, packing her equipment back into her bag and talking via the earwire to Axur, who was in his living quarters area. She didn't subvocalize; animals didn't care if she spoke out loud. "You've got a fortune in stolen and illegal pet-trade animals."

"Stolen?" The earwire made his rich baritone sound thin and distant.

"Your e-dog, for one. 'E' for enhanced. He's military-trained, and his sensory implants and command processor are still active. If you knew the passcode and comm band, you could program a percomp to give him complex sets of orders to follow, and get a feed through his implants."

"That makes sense. I named him Trouble because that's what he gets into unless I give him jobs to do. Just like some Jumpers I know."

"Your three cats are illegal because the designer spliced in a few primate genes to give them those long, flexible toes and a broader diet, and left them fertile. Any CGC health inspector would destroy them on sight, in case the splice bred true. Feed them meat and dairy, and any fruits or vegetables they'll eat. You could trade with Nuñez for some yak milk. They'll probably go into their first estrus cycle in the spring."

"Lucky they're all female. Can you or Nuñez fix their playgrounds so I don't have kittens on my hands if some equally fertile male comes looking for love?"

The big dire wolf warily poked her head into the barn's entrance. The boldest of the young cats had already left a stinging wound across her nose leather.

Bethnee laughed. "Fix their playgrounds? Yeah, we can neuter them. What did you name them?"

She held out her hand, and the wolf trotted over. She sent another thread of healing to the wound, but couldn't repair the wolf's injured dignity.

"Alpha, Bravo, and Delta. There were four, but one of them died the first day." He was silent for a long moment. *"I never liked cremation duty."*

"Me, neither." She ran her fingers through the wolf's rough coat and sighed for all the beloved animals she'd lost over the years. "Your two ravens are a non-fertile mated pair and bred to be pets, but they're about half again the standard size, and their wings are intact, so they'd be destroyed for unfair ecosystem advantage. They'll tolerate the cold, but they need clean water and bone-in meat every day, or they'll starve. There won't be enough winter carrion at this elevation. That huge aviary you built them is good, but give them more branches to sit on."

"I traded for extra cases of dog food this summer. What else do they need?"

"Grains, leftovers, especially any real meat, maybe some rotting fruit. They'll eat almost anything. You might make them some toys and puzzles with food rewards. Train them to do new tasks. Keeps their busy brains active instead of destructive."

"I named them Shade and Shadow, after that tri-D serial about thieves. I recover an amazing amount of stuff every time I clean out their bowls and baths."

She chuckled at how disgruntled he sounded. "Your foo dog, Shiza, is legal, probably stolen. They're designed to look like little curly-haired lions from pre-flight Chinese legends, but underneath, they're mostly dog, so you can feed him whatever you feed Trouble. Don't let Shiza bite you out of anger or fear. Foo dogs are designed to protect children, and his teeth can inject a nasty toxin. I can use Nuñez's lab to tailor vaccines for you and the others, as well as Nuñez and me, but it'll take a ten-day or so."

The big wolf sat on her haunches and rested her head on Bethnee's shoulder. She stroked the wolf's broad head. "Long day, huh?"

"I'm sorry, I've taken up a lot of your time."

"No, I was talking to the dire wolf. Her life is in flux at the moment, and she's in here with me, wanting affection and reassurance."

Axur mumbled something in a language she didn't recognize. Her minimal education hadn't included anything but Standard English, and whatever rude words she could pick up on the streets. *"What about the miniature dinosaur? I think it's supposed to be a stegosaurus. Its name is Ankle Biter."*

She shook her head. "I don't do reptiles, amphibians,

or fish. Can't feel them at all. Your reference manuals are your best bet. It might need to stay inside for the winter."

"Can I ask how you know so much about the pet trade? You don't seem like the type."

Ordinarily, she zeroed personal questions, but he was trusting her with the animals he loved. More tellingly, they all cared for him and trusted him without reservation.

She considered what she wanted to say. Jumpers willingly volunteered to work for the Citizen Protection Service's elite military force. The CPS hadn't done nearly as well by her, though to be fair, the huge agency had multiple missions, and it had been just the one corrupt woman.

"Never mind, it's none of my business."

"No, it's okay, it's just..." She couldn't come up with the right word. Talking about her past brought on a sour stomach and leg spasms, which was part of why she didn't do it often. "In the mandatory age-seventeen testing for minder talents, I scored high for animal-affinity minder talent. The CPS Testing Center agent *said* she got me a full scholarship at the CPS Minder Institute. Thrilled my parents, because I'd get the education they never had and couldn't afford for me. I didn't care, as long as I got to train my talent and work with animals."

"That's not what happened, I take it."

"She chemmed me, gave me an illegal chimera implant to change my DNA's biometric signature, and sent me as a counterfeit indenture to her cousin, a pet-trade dealer on a space station. She told my parents I died in a tragic interstellar passenger liner accident. Even sent them a memory diamond with my original DNA and a death payment. My bondholder made sure I knew that if I ever escaped and went home, they'd have to give back everything, which would bankrupt them."

She didn't understand Axur's reply, but the words were unmistakably curses. She envied his vocabulary.

"The first bondholder was okay. He got me training and promised I'd be a contract employee as soon as he could afford it, if I kept quiet how he got me. Three years after that, a bigger company destroyed his business and bought all his assets for a fraction. Instead of freeing me, Breitenbahn imprisoned me on an interstellar research ship. He only cared about results. I was the only 'employee' who couldn't leave, couldn't complain, couldn't fight back. And after all, I was just an indentured, subbin' minder."

Usually, she'd be shaking uncontrollably at this point, but now, she just felt queasy. Maybe it was different because Axur was just a sympathetic voice in her ear, and she was hanging on to a warm, hundred-kilo dire wolf who could sever a man's leg with a single bite.

"Breitenbahn finally made them stop abusing me when the animals started dying because I was too damaged to care for them or help the designers."

"How did you escape? I'm assuming they didn't suddenly find their lost ethics and let you go. You're far too valuable."

"Shipped myself in a container of comatose bovines bound for a remote frontier planet. It was dangerous, but Breitenbahn hired this new guard from the indenture system who wouldn't take 'no' for an answer. He shot me with an equine tranq and..." She shied away from the hideous memory. "Anyway, Nuñez was inspecting the shipment and found me. She believed my unbelievable story and took me home with her. Fed me, gave me animals to care for, made me a part of her vet business, and didn't judge. That was three years ago. I owe her more than I can ever repay."

"If I was still a Jumper, I'd invite some of my squad mates for a little vacation that just happened to coincide with the destruction of that ship."

"Thank you. I think." She smiled. "I probably shouldn't condone personal vengeance missions by elite special forces with access to really big guns and explosives."

"What can I say? We're trained to take the initiative. Lowlifes like Breitenbahn are obviously a threat to the galactic peace."

"Well, if you ever get the chance, I hope you'll let me save as many of the animals as I can. They didn't ask to be there, either."

"I'll add it to the mission parameters."

She couldn't tell if he was teasing or serious. A vigorous gust of wind rattled the doors of the barn and blew in a cloud of pine needles. "Nuñez's yaks say it'll snow tonight. Do you have someplace warm for the birds of paradise?"

"Her yaks talk? Never mind. I figured I'd bring their cage into my bunk area until I can fix up the barn."

She looked up at the roof of the chilly barn and watched the dust swirl. "I could keep them for the winter, if you like. I have geothermal heating."

"Feeding them will add to your costs. I don't want to impose."

"You aren't imposing. I offered." She gently pushed the wolf aside. "You can keep my dire wolf in trade. Give her a name. She'll love guarding you, and having the run of the valley when it snows. She's built for the cold. She'll eat a lot more than four birds, though. I'll trade removing the tracers from the rest of your animals, and a barrel of nutritional pellets that would be good for all your canines, to make it even."

In the ensuing silence, she got to her feet and brushed off her butt.

"Okay, we have a deal."

5
------

* GDAT 3241.254 *

Three months after meeting Bethnee, Axur pedaled the stationary generator cycle in his barn to give his anxiety a better outlet than churning his gut. Kivo had suddenly taken ill, and Bethnee had insisted on borrowing Nuñez's flitter and coming in person, despite a howling snowstorm. Axur had sequestered himself in the barn so as not to distract her. She'd grown more tolerant of his physical proximity in their various interactions since they'd first met, but Kivo needed her full concentration.

The earwire idea had worked so well that first day that he'd created a better, customized version for her and convinced her to wear it everywhere. It helped make up for the lost camaraderie of his fellow Jumpers, and Bethnee seemed to enjoy having someone to talk to as well. She'd dubbed it the Axur-net.

They discussed the animals, and laughed about how unprepared each of them had been to find themselves homesteading on a frontier planet. He'd at least had extensive Jumper survival training to fall back on. She grew up on city streets and had spent the last eight years in space.

Jumpers weren't good at waiting and wondering. They climbed into planetfall mech suits and kicked ass. He pedaled.

Two hours later found him adding worrying to the list of things he wasn't good at. Kivo had crashed twice, and each time, Bethnee had pulled him back from the brink. The last time she'd talked to him through the earwire, she'd sounded exhausted and distant, and she hadn't responded at all for the past ten minutes.

She was competent and smart, but something Nuñez had said one day, about a migraine headache being blowback from overusing her minder talent, had Axur thinking Bethnee might be in trouble. He wasn't trained to treat minders, because they weren't allowed in the Jumper Corps, but he was trained to treat humans. Despite what some ignorant zero-heads still thought, all minders were human. After five more minutes of plaguing himself with visions of calamity, he went back to his living quarters.

Kivo lay quietly where Axur had left him. Bethnee lay behind him, eyes closed, one arm and one knee draped loosely over him like a lover's. Kivo's breathing was steady. The tufted tip of one of his tails moved, and he swiveled one large ear toward Axur as he stepped closer.

Bethnee didn't so much as twitch, and looked pale and sweaty. If she'd been awake, she'd already be edging away.

He called her name softly, then louder, but got no response. He couldn't use his salvaged autodoc, because he didn't know how Bethnee would react to waking up in an enclosed cylinder little bigger than a cremation tube. That left his bed, which easily held him and various pets, so it wouldn't make her claustrophobic.

He gently extracted her from around Kivo and carried her toward the back room. She felt warmly female in his arms. He felt guilty even thinking it, because it would terrify her. He had no business wanting a woman who'd been treated as a subhuman, and beaten or worse to force compliance. Hell, the thoughts terrified him. He was the opposite of attractive, and had enough baggage of his own to open a tourist shop at the spaceport. He couldn't see how it would end well for either of them.

She began to convulse just as he got her to the bedroom door. He let her legs drop so she could throw up without hurting herself, but he couldn't catch enough of the mess with his cybernetic hand to keep it from soaking her shirt and pants. The stomach-churning smell assaulted his nose, but as a former battlefield medic and current household servant to nine pets, he was used to dealing with all sorts of unpleasant odors and substances.

By the time he got her into the fresher, she was barely responsive.

He sprayed her off as best he could, but she wasn't wearing her waterproof work tunic, and was soon soaked and shivering.

Telling himself he was looking but not seeing, he removed everything but her underwear, then draped her with one of his blankets and carried her to his bed. He quickly found her veterinary scanner and used it on her.

And since he was already being unethical by examining her without her permission, he evaluated her bad left leg, with its deep, ugly scars and distorted tendons and muscles. He swore in several languages as he dressed her in one of his tunics, then covered her up with more blankets. Since she had been a Concordance citizen, her kidnappers—he refused to call them bondholders—could have had her injury fixed for free anywhere in the Concordance. They'd purposefully left her untreated for years.

He couldn't ever return to the Jumpers again, and he was in no position to organize a mission against Bethnee's captors, but he did send a fervent prayer out to the constant stars to exact the justice he couldn't.

6

Bethnee woke to unfamiliar... everything. The soft glowlight on the wall, the cat purring on her chest, the furry body at her side, the too-long sleeve of her shirt. Not to mention, a room that looked like the shell of an interstellar ship's stateroom.

The bed shifted, and a golden furry face appeared above hers.

"Hello, Trouble." Her voice sounded raspy and her throat hurt. The dog licked at her cheek, then pushed off from the bed and left.

The furry warmth at her side stirred. Shiza, the square-jawed foo dog with the perpetual cute grimace and drooling habit, scrambled to his feet and shook himself, leaving a drifting cloud of curly golden fur.

Bethnee cautiously reached out with her talent to Delta, the cat on her chest, just to make sure she could. She'd exhausted all her reserves to save Kivo because she knew how much Axur loved the beast. She didn't even know if she'd succeeded. Or what time it was. Or how she came to be mostly naked in Axur's big bed. That realization made her feel aware, but not wary. She put the thought aside for later.

She sat up and discovered a veterinary fluids pump attached to the back of her hand. She was still staring at it stupidly when Axur appeared at the bedroom door.

"How do you feel?" He touched a control on the wall to make the lights brighter.

"Like hammered horse shi... " She trailed off as she got a good look at Axur. She'd never seen him without winter clothes and his heavy cloak, and now there he stood, damp and naked except for the towel around his trim waist and defined abdominals. He'd tied back the coiled strands of his long, frizzy hair, revealing a well-muscled chest that was a blend of warm brown skin, a few scars to give it character, and a smooth transition to his cybernetic arm, with its mismatched synthskin patches and exposed biometal. "You're stunning."

He blinked, clearly nonplussed.

"Sorry." She couldn't stop staring. Didn't want to, in fact. "From the way you talk, I'd thought you looked like a corroded, spare-parts cyborg from the serial sagas." That was probably the lamest thing she'd ever said. "Sorry. I'll shut up now."

He started to speak, but stopped himself. He seemed not to know what to do with his hands. "I'm not standing too close?"

"No." She tried to puzzle it out. Humans usually felt like phantoms to her, like she was listening to the wrong frequency. "Maybe I'm still being affected by talent blowback sickness, but right now, you're not a ghost, you're solid. Like one of Nuñez's yaks."

He laughed out loud.

She shrugged, embarrassed. "Sorry."

"I'm flattered. Truly." His warm smile made her believe it. "Back to my original question. Your color is much better, and your temperature stabilized a while ago. How are you?"

"I'll live. How's Kivo?"

"See for yourself." He turned aside, and Kivo stepped forward, looking as healthy as she'd ever seen him. Relief flooded through her. He launched himself toward her to put his first set of paws on the bed and joyfully lick her face.

"Yes, all right." She rubbed his ears. "I'm happy to see you're alive, too." The aches in all her joints and the post-fever lethargy melted away at the affection Kivo was broadcasting. In that moment, she could readily believe Axur's theory that Kivo was an empath, just like Nuñez.

"I cleaned your clothes. Your earwire and percomp are on the table."

She had a hazy memory of a brightly lit room, and throwing up. "What time is it?"

"Eleven thirteen. Should be light out, but you can barely tell through the nonstop snow." At their latitude and a ten-day from the winter solstice, they got less than five hours of sun per day.

She was loath to leave the soft comfort of Axur's loving pets and his big bed, but she'd already kept him from it for ten hours, and she had to return Nuñez's flitter and get home. "Could I impose on you for the use of your fresher and something to eat?"

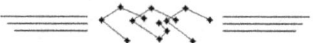

"PLEASE DON'T KILL ME, but while you were unconscious, I examined your bad leg." Axur sat at the other end of his small couch and sipped coffee from a large mug.

A flare of unease spiked, but she smothered it. Nothing had happened. Axur was her kind, funny friend who talked to her every day. He wasn't a brutal man who drugged her and inflicted degradation and pain. Axur was a warm, strong, stolid yak. "And?"

"Completely repairable in any medical center with tissue-cloning facilities."

"And completely unaffordable. Homesteaders like me have to pay hard credit. Even settlers like Nuñez have to co-pay. This isn't the Concordance, yet." The swirling snow outside the window made her feel cold. She wasn't used to windows. "I have a better chance of winning the galactic lottery. Or I would, if I had enough hard credit to buy a ticket."

"I know, so I have a deal for you. You give me Serena permanently, and come every ten-day to check on my pets and help me with two-person jobs. In exchange, I'll design a procedure my autodoc can handle to reattach the torn ligament and repair the lateral quadriceps muscle that gives you the most grief. You'd have to stay off it for the day and eat a lot to compensate for the rapid-heal, but it should improve your mobility and strength."

Her jaw dropped. "You have an *autodoc*?"

"Yeah, it came with the freighter. Running low on basic chems and anesthetics, though. I'll need more afterward."

"Holy hells. Do you have any idea what a working autodoc is worth? And with your medic training and language skills? Nuñez was right. You don't have to hide up here. Move into town, and they'd build you the clinic of your dreams. The settlement company couldn't stop them or even take a cut."

A grim look settled on his face. "I can't." The conviction in his tone left no room for argument.

She would have liked to point out that he was obviously lonely, based on how often he pinged her just to chat, but he knew what he could and couldn't do. She disliked it when Nuñez pushed her, so she wasn't going to do that to her only other friend on the planet.

"You'll need your autodoc supplies for yourself, so no deal on that. I'll take the rest of the trade, though— Serena for the extra pair of hands and veterinary care." The wolf in question was out in the blizzard, frolicking like she was a spring-loaded mountain goat instead of a dignified guardian. "Your place is better for her than mine."

He frowned and reached for his cup, but stopped to examine the exposed biometal knuckles of his cybernetic hand.

She moved Shiza, the warmth-seeking foo dog, off her lap, then stood and stepped into her boots. Alpha, the darkest cat, helped by batting at the decorative lacings. Beta jumped her, Delta jumped Beta, and a battle royale ensued. It was a wonder Axur's living quarters weren't a constant shamble.

She glanced at Axur, expecting to see him smiling at his silly cats, but he was looking up at her pensively.

"Ever heard of a Citizen Protection Service black-box project?"

"Er, maybe?" She dredged up the memory. "Something about secret weapons?"

"I am one."

She had no idea what he was talking about, but his bleak expression made her want to comfort him. "Because of your cybernetics? Lots of Jumpers have those, don't they? You can't all be weapons."

"Because of what's *in* my cybernetics. The CPS secretly 'volunteered' me for a research group's project that turned me into a continually broadcasting comm unit. I could probably uplink directly to the high-orbit galactic comms buoy from here."

"I'm sorry, I'm not following." She touched the earwire he'd given her and convinced her to wear, even when sleeping. "Is that how you made the Axur-net?"

He stood and turned to her, shoving his hands in his pockets. If she took one step closer, she could almost touch him. It was the closest she'd been to him without the fear taking over her motor control to make her tremble with the imperative to run, to hide. She gave herself a mental shake to refocus on what Axur was saying.

"...first in my squad to try out the new, better battery in my cybernetic legs. I woke up in a space station in a high-security research clinic, with a new cybernetic arm that I didn't need, and a satellite uplink built into me. The assholes stole me and altered the records to make it look like I'd voluntarily signed on for their research project. They told me their goal was to improve field communications for Jumpers, but I soon figured out the real purpose was to intercept, decrypt, and twist enemy comms."

Her sluggish brain finally put together a piece of the puzzle. "Your cloak. It blocks your broadcast." She looked around at Axur's quarters, made out of the pieces of an interstellar ship. "This is incalloy, for transit space. That's why you don't have to cover up in here."

"Yeah. I added a countervalent grid, powered by the ship's thousand-year batteries. It scatters my signal."

"Why do you need to?"

"Because ten months ago, I stole this freighter and escaped. The CPS wants me back, and not to return me to my squad." He held up his cybernetic hand and made a fist. "I'm still tuned up to enhanced Jumper speed and strength, which is illegal outside the Corps. I really am a cyborg. Point is, my cybernetics have enough experimental nanotech to buy Del'Arche's entire settlement debt. I'm the only survivor of ten other 'volunteers.'" He rocked on his heels. "When my signal pings any official comm system, the system records my unique comm signature. If that got back to the main Concordance net, it would likely trigger a galaxy-wide detain-and-restrain order on me that says I'm dangerously delusional, and offers a juicy reward to keep me iced until the fastest CPS cruiser can get here."

"I'm sorry, Axur. That farkin' flatlines." She didn't know what else to say. No minder talent in the universe could change the past, and she didn't know any minder forecasters who could advise him on how to improve his future. She limped to her vet bag on the table to check that it was sealed tight.

Axur grabbed his coat and step into his combat-style boots. "I'll clear the path again and warm up the flitter."

She eyed his everyday work pants. "Do your legs feel cold?"

"No, they're internally heated to normal body temperature. My processor interface tells me what the external temperature is." He smiled ruefully. "My ass and dangly bits get cold, though."

She laughed at his phrasing. He had the oddest euphemisms for genitalia.

He bunched his hair on top of his head so he could slip on his fancy transparent snow hood. "Some Jumpers choose to have the full input-to-nerve mapping done, to make the synthskin and cybernetics feel as real as possible, but I know the endocrine system isn't there, and I didn't want to be distracted by phantom sensations." He flexed his cybernetic hand. "The researchers did it for my arm without asking what I wanted. After I landed, I had to hack into my own processor to make it quit telling me about the burns. Even though I have the key, it took me days because of the evolving cryptogon."

He lifted his heavy cloak and pushed his head through the round opening, then sealed it. "I'll be on earwire."

He slid open the door to reveal a snow-covered wolf, who danced back in excitement when she realized Axur was coming outside.

His tone signaled in her earwire. *"Feel free to raid the*

cabinets or cold box if you're still hungry. You had a stressful night."Heavy breaths of exertion punctuated his words.

"I'm good. I've been looking at your decor. Very mad techno. Did they teach you that in Jumper school?"

"Some. I learn languages more quickly when I busy my hands. The CPS researchers gave me comm specialist courses, and started training me to use the new tech I'm carrying. Even trained me how to repair my cybernetics. When they gave me control during testing and forgot to turn it off over lunch, I cracked their internal security and read everything, not just the sanitized version they gave me, which is how I found out about the nine other test-subject fatalities. I sure as hell didn't want to be number ten."

"I'm glad you escaped." As she said the words, she realized her life would be immeasurably less interesting without Axur in it. Because he wasn't there in front of her, it was easier to ask the question that had been bothering her. "Are you staying away from Tanimai because you're afraid someone in town would betray you to the CPS?" Someone like Nuñez, or her.

"No. If and when the CPS captures me, they wouldn't care who they else hurt, including anyone they thought I'd shared secrets with. Out here, they only catch me, and leave the town alone."

The implications of his story sank in. "You're just like Kivo. You're a failed experiment they want to dissect." She took his silence to mean he'd already thought of that. "Why did you tell me all this now?"

The answer was a long time in coming.

"Because if you come up here someday and I'm gone, I wanted you to know that it wasn't my choice."

The thought of losing him to that fate terrified her worse than the fear response when the man got too close. And if that wasn't a complete contradiction, she didn't know what was. She felt like she ought to say something. "I would take care of your animals."

"Thank you. They're my family."

"Don't you have any of your own?" Not that he could go home while he was still a fugitive, but maybe he could see them again someday. People lived to a hundred and seventy and more with modern medicine.

"Dead. Con-Kella Pandemic of 3215. I was raised in group homes. The Jumper Corps became my family after that. What about you?"

"Only child, or at least I was. My parents worked long hours and left me home a lot. I made friends with every stray animal in the neighborhood, and figured I'd work at a rescue shelter." She gave a self-deprecatory laugh. "And look at me now, on top of the world."

"I'm at the barn. I'll send Serena to walk you down to the flitter."

"Okay." She took a deep breath and spoke before she lost her nerve. "You could come with me."

"Why, are you feeling sick?"

"No, it's just... I don't... You should..." The unexpected rise of emotion tangled her tongue. "My place is hard to find and well protected. If I show you where it is, and you need somewhere to hide, you could go there."

The silence stretched. She wished she could see his face, because maybe he wasn't interested, or thought the idea was lame.

"Okay."

AN HOUR LATER, she landed the flitter on the snow-dusted gravel of her homestead's landing pad. Nuñez had told her to keep the flitter until the next day. The storm had finally stopped, but left deep snow behind.

Bethnee checked her security system's activity monitor, then opened the flitter doors. She collected her kit, locked the doors, and caught Axur's eye. "Stay on my trail so you don't get lost."

She led the way up the path to her home. Under the obscuring snow, it looked like ramshackle stacks of logs between a cluster of tall boulders. Kivo whined excitedly as she opened her front door and led him and Axur-the-yak inside. He was only her second human visitor. She'd have never believed she'd ever allow a man into her house if she hadn't been living it at that moment.

She turned on the lights, then pointed to the hooks by the door. "Hang your stuff there."

She'd already sent her talent out to her animals to tell them she was coming, and warn them about the stranger. Axur's tribe comprised extraordinary, valuable pets. Hers were civilization's discards, like her.

After Axur wrestled off his coat while leaving his shielding cloak in place, he stepped into the cabin's common area to look around. She'd purposefully left this part of her home looking primitive and half-dilapidated to fool any would-be intruders. She saw on his face the moment he started noticing the little features that would make an uninvited guest's life miserable.

"Impressive." He gave her a sly smile. "I'm glad I'm not your enemy."

"There's more outside. I'll show you before dark. I add to them when I get a new idea. I need a place to feel safe."

"Copy that." He tilted his head toward the back, hidden in shadows. "That where you really live?"

"Yeah, come on back."

7

* GDAT 3241.255 *

Axur decided that calling Bethnee's place a cave was like calling Kivo a pet—true as far as it went, but a wholly inadequate description. The log cabin front concealed the sealed entrance to an extensive cave system. Its main feature was a subterranean hot spring that she'd taken full advantage of to create habitats for herself and her animals. He especially envied the temperature-regulated pool she'd built by shaping a natural depression in the cave and installing a series of pumps and pipes.

Until he saw her relaxed in her own environment, he never realized how effectively she hid her vibrancy and unconventional beauty. She'd even come within centimeters of him a couple of times without flinching. A strong desire to touch her and be touched back arced through him. He locked his knees and shoved his fists in his pockets under his poncho. It wasn't just general lust, because he didn't want physical affection from the other women he'd interacted with in town, and males didn't flux his drive. He shouldn't have agreed to come, but loneliness and longing overrode his reservations.

He shoved his conflict into the frustratingly large box of things he couldn't control and focused on something he could. "So, I've met everyone except Jynx."

Bethnee grinned. "I saved her for last, because you'll like her best."

"It'll be hard to top a white weasel trained to steal." He pointed toward her indoor garden, which she'd created by widening a natural cave cathedral and piping in circulating hot water and air. "Not to mention, an indoor bamboo forest to keep a half-blind red panda happy."

"Come see."

She took him through a narrow, curving corridor that led to a noticeably cooler part of the cave. The near-frosty air was a shock after the heat of the garden. Kivo's attention was riveted on the tall rows of stacked crates along the wall.

From between an opening in the stacks, a fully-grown snow leopard padded in. She glanced once at him and Kivo in seeming boredom as she gracefully jumped up onto the battered table. She sat and curled her long tail around her, watching Bethnee.

He started to speak, but froze when he was interrupted by a low, rusty-sounding half-growl from Jynx. "Uhm, is she torqued?"

Bethnee laughed as she stretched a hand out and moved closer to sink her fingers into the thick fur on the cat's neck. "No, that's just her 'hello.' It's called chuffing. You can come closer. It's a dirty little secret in the planet terraform industry that the last of the snow leopards died in a zoo long before First Flight, and that all the 'naturals' are actually recreations. She's designer, not feral. I've let her know that you and Kivo are my friends."

He edged closer, trying not to stress Bethnee but wanting a better look at the big cat's left front leg. "I've never seen an animal with cybernetics." The cat's distinctive spotted fur ended with a ragged transition to the raw, articulated biometal model of a cat's leg. The toes on the wide paw had lethal biometal claws. If she'd ever had synthskin—synthfur?—it was gone now.

"And you probably won't see another. Animal brains usually reject the motile processor input, even with complete nerve mapping and fluid sync. She's unique, and worth a fortune." Jynx chuffed again, showing her sharp carnivore's teeth. "Nuñez found her at the spaceport, wrapped like a mummy, half-dead, in a secret compartment of a large-animal container." Bethnee chuckled. "The yaks get nervous just smelling her, so Nuñez gave her to me. Besides, her visible biometal makes her a theft magnet. I can't let her go out very often."

Following instinct, Axur held out both his human and cybernetic hands for Jynx to smell. He smiled when she rubbed her head on both, marking him with her scent. "Cats are cats."

"Yep." She leaned her hip against the table. "I had a devious reason for inviting you here."

He grinned at her. "You're the least devious person I know."

She snorted. "I'm the least *tactful* person you know. There's a difference." She pushed a stray lock of dark hair behind her ear. His fingers tingled with the desire to find out if it felt as silky as it looked. "I was hoping you'd look at Jynx's cybernetic biometal-to-bone interface and tell me what needs fixing. When she jumps down from more than a few meters, her shoulder collapses, and now she's afraid of going up high." She pointed to mountain of crates. "I had to move her den down to floor level, and that makes her nervous."

"I'm willing," he said dubiously, "but I know absolute zero about leopard anatomy. We'd have to take her back to my place for the tools and computers. And even then, her cybernetics might be a whole different design."

"If we pool our skills and talents, I'd sure like to try." She rubbed Jynx's ear. "Humans have treated her so badly. She deserves the best life I can give her."

He'd have given anything to take Bethnee's sadness away, but he'd used up his lifetime quota of miracles when he'd escaped the CPS researchers. He shoved his hands in his pockets. "Whenever you're ready."

FOUR DAYS LATER, Axur quickly carried forty kilos of chemmed snow leopard to the temporary exam table he'd rigged in his workroom. Jynx had made a bad jump the day before and was in constant pain.

Bethnee looked everywhere but him. "Did this room used to be the nav pod?" Her hands trembled when she wasn't focused on the leopard.

"Yes." He hunched over to lay Jynx on her side on the folded blankets. He maneuvered around to the other side of the table. "The landing drilled the freighter halfway into the mountain, so I took advantage of it and dug in more." He smiled. "I didn't win the hot-spring lottery like you did."

He pulled the big tech scanner down close to the leopard's leg. "We're in luck. She's got a hidden jackwire port at the shoulder interface." He pulled one of his longwires from the tray and held it out to Bethnee. "I'll show you where, if you'll insert it. When I run a diagnostic, tell me if it hurts her."

She bent close and inserted the wire with a steady hand. "Go."

He touched a control and watched the readout. "Standard processor, zero security. They must not have expected to lose her." He frowned. "Battery is old-*old* style, and running low." He looked at Bethnee. "I don't know how your talent works, but can you check the interface area for temperature? Her processor is conserving battery power by reducing the leg's internal heat generation. Probably feels like she's constantly cold." He put his human hand on Jynx's shoulder at the interface to see if he could feel the difference.

Bethnee's eyes lost focus, a sign she was using her talent. "It feels numb to her, but it always has. I thought that was normal." She frowned. "Damn, I think I missed a passive tracer, right at the interface. The cybernetics must have masked it."

He moved his hand aside so she could lean over and probe with delicate fingers.

"It's faint..." Her voice trailed off, and she straightened abruptly. "It's in *your* hand."

"What?" He held up his hand and flexed his fingers. "Frelling hell. I removed the standard Jumper tracers and the extras in my cybernetics. I never thought to look elsewhere."

"You might have missed them, anyway. It's pet grade. Tiny." She shook her head. "I don't know why, but ever since I healed Kivo, you've felt real to me, not like a ghost. I think I could tell you where the tracers are, if I get close enough." She blew out a loud breath and looked at her shaking hands. "And if I don't flatline." She crossed her arms and shoved her hands under her armpits.

Just great. The woman he most wanted to get close to was terrified at the thought of even touching him. "Let's deal with Jynx first."

THE FIX WAS easy to describe—replace Jynx's failing battery with one of his spares—and hard to achieve. What would have been a ten-minute procedure in a Jumper med center turned into three hours of guesswork and improvisation using repurposed equipment in his temporary lab. The trickiest part had been helping Jynx interpret and accept the full input from her cybernetic processor.

Axur triggered two mealpacks as Bethnee encouraged the leopard to walk in circles around the couch.

He eyed the weather through his only window. "We could take Jynx outside after lunch."

"Good." Bethnee smiled. "She's just humoring me,

walking around in here. Thanks for giving up one of your batteries. At full strength, she's amazing."

"It's a good cause." He wanted to tell Bethnee she was amazing, with her courage to fight through debilitating post-trauma stress to help her pets and his, but didn't think she'd like the reminder. He pushed the heated tray across the counter toward her. "I'm glad the freighter had enough mealpacks for a decade, but I'm looking forward to growing season again. I was lucky the freighter was shipping seed starts and had a superb library in the shipcomp."

"I want to create a hydroponic garden." She crossed to the counter and pulled out the mealpack's utensils. "If it works for starships, it should work for the cave."

"I can print small flexible parts for you, like nozzles and connectors, if you can trade for lexo substrate."

She nearly choked. "You have a working *printer*?" She set her fork down and stared at him. "The only other printer within a hundred kilometers is owned by the settlement company, and they only take hard credit. You could trade for anything you wanted. *Anything*."

"I had no idea." Once again, he was surprised at all the things he'd taken for granted in his former life.

She frowned. "Actually, you might want to keep quiet until you read the settlement contract's sections on salvage rights. Nuñez sent you a copy, didn't she?"

He nodded. "Yes." He'd only read the part about homesteading, which said if he could improve a perimeter-marked plot of land for two years, it became his, and conferred legal resident status with it. If the company caught him before that, they'd haul him into the

Concordance and charge him with trespass. And that was only if the relentless CPS didn't find him first.

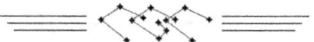

AXUR WOULD BET hard credit that he and Bethnee were the only two people in the galaxy who had ever seen a cybernetic snow leopard and a formidable dire wolf play tag in the deep snow.

Bethnee laughed when Jynx made an astonishing six-meter leap onto a boulder to avoid Serena's lunge. He snuck a glance at Bethnee, enjoying her happiness. "Are you helping them get along?" He tapped his temple, to indicate her enviable minder talent.

"A little. Mostly Jynx, because this isn't her territory."

He checked his internal chrono. "We better start collecting your gear, and I need to check the barn." He pointed a thumb toward Jynx. "I'll send Trouble out to keep an eye on these two." Axur had yet to be able to crack the encryption on the e-dog's command processor that Bethnee had told him about, but he kept trying.

Back in his living quarters, he found Bethnee leaning against the kitchen counter, holding her small veterinary surgical suite. "I'd like to try removing your tracers."

He blinked in surprise. "Now? Are you sure?"

"Hell, no, but it'll be worse if I give myself time to think about it." She searched his face. "Unless you don't trust me?"

"I trust you with anything except making coffee. Where do you want me?"

"Chair, I guess."

He hesitated, then pulled off his shirt and sat. "Let's try this first." Jumpers gave up caring about nudity in the first ten-day of training, but she might not be so comfortable, especially considering his gender. He held out his hand.

She opened the suite, exposing the instrumented interior, then swallowed visibly and took slow steps toward him. "Talk to me. Tell me how you escaped the shitheads who put tracers in you like you were a lab animal." She rested trembling, cool fingertips on the back of his hand. "I like the sound of your voice."

He described how he made off with hoarded supplies, including extra batteries and tools, and hijacked the freighter. A lucky torpedo right before he went transit forced him to reprogram the navcomp on the fly to exit at Del'Arche, where he skidded in on a failing system drive and scorched, cracked atmosphere wings. He used the debris to build his shelter.

She trembled the whole time, but she found and excised the tracers in his wrist, upper arm, and both of his shoulder blades. The surgical suite made it quick and nearly painless. The tracers under his collarbones were harder for both of them. Tremors wracked her, but she stuck to her task. He closed his eyes, but the butterfly touch of her cool fingers and the warm female scent of her saturated his senses. He could no more prevent his erection than he could prevent his satellite uplink from broadcasting. He prayed to the constant stars she wouldn't notice, or he'd never see her again.

When the suite sounded its completion chime, she pulled it off and lurched toward the front door to slide it open. She panted like she'd been running low on oxygen in her space exosuit.

After a moment of indecision, Axur climbed to his feet and pulled on his shirt, letting it hang loose over the front of his pants.

She turned back to him, looking pale and exhausted. "Sorry. I'm a warped mess." She brushed a strand of hair behind her ear. "You've got four more." A tear fell. She brushed it away absently.

"That's enough for today. If the CPS is close enough to ping-trace the rest of them, I'm as good as iced, anyway." He picked up the crate with the rest of her supplies. "No need to apologize for negative stress feedback. I've had it, and it's no less debilitating because it's just in your mind. Jumpers are lucky enough to get quick support and professional treatment from top-level minders and medics."

She gave him a watery smile. "I thought you said Jumpers ate pain for breakfast."

"We do. But we acknowledge the pain for each other, so no one has to carry it alone." He took a deep breath and let it out slowly, hoping to drain off the anger he felt at what he'd lost, what they'd both lost. "We look out for each other, because no one else will."

---

8

* GDAT 3241.264 *

A hard fall off her glide board onto her bad leg left Bethnee barely hobbling as she let herself into her cabin. The added weight of her vetmed kit brought clawing pain with every step as she re-armed the security systems and checked the logs and the analog telltales. No one had bothered her in the two years she'd lived there, but carelessness was no longer in her nature.

She made halting progress to the cave's kitchen, escorted by her pets. She couldn't afford to be disabled, or she and the animals would go hungry. She wished Axur hadn't suggested they try to heal her leg with the autodoc, because she was tempted to take him up on the offer.

It had been five days since she and Axur had fixed Jynx —and since Bethnee had failed to finish removing the tracers from Axur. He pinged her that night and since, as if nothing had changed. Maybe it hadn't for him, but her world had tilted on its axis.

She'd willingly touched a warm, half-naked man. Her dark, horrific memories had lost some of their power. Maybe it was time and distance, but more likely, it was the healing balm of Axur. Handsome, resilient, clever, caring Axur, who resurrected memories of her younger days when sex was sweet and teenage dreams brimmed with passion and romance. Those memories used to belong to a forgotten stranger, but she could almost believe they were hers again.

Most of her reaction when she'd removed the tracers had been fighting the impulse to touch him, like a lover. It scared and exhilarated her. And the realization that he'd been sexually aroused by skinny, scarred her had made her almost forget to breathe. She'd let him think she was still afraid because he was a man with the power to break her body, when the truth was, she was newly terrified that he had the power to shatter her heart.

She could remain silent and maintain the friendly status quo, but could she live with herself if she did? She wasn't Jumper brave, but she'd worked so hard not to let fear rule her. It wasn't fair to either of them for her to stand in the doorway like a cat, neither going all the way out or in. She didn't know what he wanted, but she'd never find out if she didn't ask. She tapped her Axur-net earwire and waited for his response.

"Hey. I'm glad you pinged. I have an idea for fixing my broadcasting comms problem, but I need your help."

His voice sounded like he was right next to her, whispering into her ear, making her stomach flutter.

"Sure." She took a deep, steadying breath. "What do you want in trade to use your autodoc to fix my leg?"

THE WEAK WINTER sun turned the snow glossy as Bethnee looked out the window of Axur's home. She hated being a patient, but knew she'd be just as attentive if Nuñez or Axur got hurt, so she accepted his coddling. In moderation.

"I thought I told you to stay off the leg," said Axur.

She turned to watch as he rolled in a cart filled with tools and equipment. "I hopped."

He rolled his eyes. "You're worse than a combat Jumper." He pointed to the chair and footrest he'd rigged for her. "Sit."

She hopped back and eased herself down. "It's boring."

"Yeah, well, that's why you're going to help me crack my second processor." He pushed the cart next to her chair, then put his stool next to it. "You need to eat like a Jumper today. Are you hungry yet?"

"No. Shaky, though."

"Am I too close?" He started to move the stool, but she put her hand on it.

"No." She pointed to the space just in front of her. "Sit and tell me what you want me to do." When he hesitated, she added, "You're still a yak."

He sat, watching her carefully as he did. She sent out a thread of talent to him, letting the solid strength of him fill her senses. Her new strategy had worked so far, even when she'd been pantless in front of him and needed his help to lift her badly bruised leg into the autodoc. Admittedly, she'd had to reach for the minds of the trusting animals to remind her brain how to stay calm, but she still put it in the win column.

"Yesterday, I finally cracked Trouble's command module security. Mine looks similar." He held up a small hexagon-shaped percomp and a longwire. "I'm going to jack in, but if I trip the kill switch the researchers contantly threatened me with, I'll need you to reinitialize me. I'll show you how."

"It's sweet of you to not see me as a technological flatliner, but we both know the truth." She stifled an impulse to reach out and stroke his arm.

"That's why I'm going to show you. I stayed up last night and built some routines to try if the normal sequence fails." He opened a flat display and pointed to a long list. "They're in order of what I think you should try first, but I added notes about what they do, so you can use your judgment."

"You did all this last night?" She knew he was a get-it-done kind of person—probably all Jumpers were—but this seemed excessive. "Why the rush?"

He looked away from her, then back. "It's like you said. I'm hiding up here. Letting my limitations imprison me as much as the researchers did. I only see you and Nuñez, and a few townspeople for trades. I was good at being a Jumper, but that's gone, so I need a new career."

The thought of losing him burned like a beamer through her heart, but she couldn't begrudge him his freedom, any more than she could begrudge Jynx enjoying her recovered strength and agility. Axur's premium skills and valuable ship contents meant he could move to a warm southern city. After what the Citizen Protection

Service had done to him, he deserved more than a quirky little town of misfits and a damaged, graceless woman who thought of him as a yak.

"Okay," she said. "Show me what to do."

"I'm in! My uplink controller isn't just similar to Trouble's, it's the exact same model, just customized."

It had taken Axur over forty minutes to explain all the contingencies he'd come up with, and less than ten minutes to crack his system on the first try. His whoop startled the cats and made Kivo dance in excitement.

"Congratulations." She couldn't help but smile in response to his delight. "Once I extract your other tracers, you can be truly free." Her bad leg was pins and needles, like she'd run into a cactus, but she'd take that over weak and numb. She slid her leg off the footrest and ignored the wave of wooziness that washed over her when she sat up too fast. "Fresher first, though."

"I'll get your crutches." He stood and gave her a stern look. "Stay put."

The natural light from the window made a bronze halo of his frizzy hair, which he'd grown to make him less recognizable. His short, darker beard highlighted his strong jaw. His thin knit shirt stretched across his wide shoulders and muscled chest, giving her the urge to snuggle against his warmth. She smiled up at him. "You're an impossibly gorgeous man."

He gave her an assessing look. "I think you're reacting abnormally to the recovery chems."

"Maybe," she conceded. "Normal and I have rarely been on speaking terms." A warm sensation flushed through her and pooled in her pelvis. "I think I could kiss you right now, and not even twitch." She lifted her rock-steady hand up to him in invitation and smiled. "Want to experiment? It'd be for science."

"No," he said firmly. "Not that I don't want to kiss you, because I do, more than you know, but you are nowhere near capable of consent right now." He backed away and shoved his hands in his pockets, making his shoulders and pectoral muscles flex deliciously. "If you still want to kiss me tomorrow, we'll talk about it."

THE AFTERNOON PASSED in a blur as she alternately ate snacks and dozed on the couch. She was soon victimized by small animals that wanted a warm body to sleep on or next to. She dreamily watched him solving the mysteries of his uplink, thinking him brilliant and sexy, wishing she weren't too impaired to savor the holiday from her responsibilities and her fears.

She finally woke and sat up around the time he was serving dinner. "Am I allowed to try walking now?" She massaged her thigh gently. "I have more sensation in the lateral muscle than I've had in years."

"That depends. Are you still dizzy?" He gave her a sardonic smile. "Do you still want to kiss me?"

She met his query with a steady gaze. "No, and yes."

He drew a surprised breath, then shook his head. "Use the crutches. Your brain isn't exactly green-go right now."

She sighed, knowing he was probably right. Even if the weird chems reaction temporarily freed her to act on her desire to invite herself into his bed for a hot connect, it wouldn't be pleasant for either of them when her old fears came back online the next morning.

She levered herself up onto the crutches and made her way to the fresher, where they'd put her overnight bag to keep it safe from critters. When she returned, she put a package in front of him. "Happy Solstice Day." She triggered her mealpack's heater.

He blinked in surprise, darting his glance between her and the package. His smile grew as he untied the twine and opened it. "Real coffee!" He held the cloth bag to his nose and took in the scent appreciatively. He held up the other gift. "What's on the longwire?"

"Common and relic language courses." She pulled out the utensils from her mealpack. "You said you don't have anyone to practice with. I only know Standard English and one city's street slang, and Nuñez has mostly forgotten her family's Tagalog, so I traded for the courses whenever I treated pets. You can help me expand my horizons. I need more swear words."

He smiled as he put the longwire in his shirt pocket and patted it. "Thank you."

Seeing how much the simple gifts pleased him, she vowed to give him as many as she could before he left for wider, warmer pastures. She must still be farked by the chems, because the thought made her want to hug him tight and cry on his broad shoulder.

He triggered the heater on his mealpack. "I have

presents for you and Nuñez, too." Something on his cart beeped, and he grinned. "Excuse me a minute."

Axur returned with a small percomp strapped to his cybernetic wrist, and removed a disgruntled cat from his chair so he could sit. Beta promptly jumped into Bethnee's lap and settled.

"Okay," she said. "Remember that I'm tech illiterate, and explain to me what you've been doing. I think I'm finally awake enough to keep it straight."

"I downloaded copies of my processor and controller software, so I could test things on the comp instead of me." He pointed a thumb to his equipment cart. "Luckily, I exited the CPS research program earlier than they planned, so my tech's code isn't encrypted. The downside is, not everything works right, and they'd only just started training me on how to use it. I'll need time to reverse-engineer it and figure out what I can do."

He talked between bites. "I turned off the uplink. I'll be glad to retire my poncho. Then I purged my unique comm signature from the dozens of dataspaces they squirreled it away."

She nodded. "Sounds like the tech equivalent of the tracers."

"Yeah, that's me, valuable research animal." He finished the entrée portion of his meal in three shoveling bites. "I just finished a prog that'll let me uplink with whatever signature I want and control it with the cybernetic interface in my ocular implant. Next, I have to figure out how to twist the planetary geomarkers."

"Twist them?" She frowned. "Won't that mess up navigation around here?"

"No, not the geomarkers themselves, just the ping refs that go with my signal. Most comms satellites record signal origination data along with the unique ID. It'd be suspicious if a flurry of new IDs all came from outside one tiny mountain town, or with no refs at all. At the very least, it'd trigger a settlement company audit, which would *not* make me popular in Tanimai. I don't want my activities to trace back to anyone here."

"Why? What are you going to do?"

"Download every hypercube of data and AI analysis from the orbiting weather system. Technically, it belongs to the Del'Arche government." He scooped up the empty mealpack trays. "You said the satellite network was malfing at the time, but I want to look for evidence of my unexpected planetfall."

She chuckled. "Is that what Jumpers call a crash landing?"

A corner of his mouth twitched in humor. "Dull mission reports mean no unwanted attention from High Command." He glanced at her crutches on the floor. "Want to try walking?"

She took a deep breath. "Yeah, but first, I want to take advantage of what the recovery drugs have done to me, so I can finish getting the tracers out of you."

9

"Now?" It would mean getting naked for her. His hormones were instantly on board, which was exactly why it was a bad idea. His unavoidable erection and obvious desire would likely traumatize her, recovery-drug high or not. If he ever hoped to take their relationship to a deeper level, she needed time.

He took a breath, held it, and let it out. "I think we should let Nuñez do it."

"I'm not..." She trailed off. "Okay." She looked away and dropped her head.

He knew he'd hurt her feelings, but didn't know how to fix it.

She stood up slowly, using the back of the chair for support. She rocked from side to side, as if testing her balance. "Feels weird. Strong, but weird." She started to take a step, then looked down at her feet with a frown. "I think I'm going to have to learn how to walk again."

"When they fit Jumpers with cybernetics, the physical terrorists tell us not to think about the mechanics, just focus on the intent to get somewhere."

"The whats?" She laughed. "Oh. Therapists." She turned. "I'll walk in here."

"Good." He watched Bethnee limp her way around the couch several times. "Are you limping because you have to, or out of habit?"

She stopped and looked at her legs. "Beats me." She shrugged. "I'll let you know tomorrow morning when we walk down to the flitter."

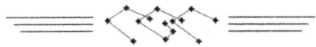

THE SATELLITE DATA he downloaded overnight was good, bad, and interesting. The network had indeed been offline for maintenance and hadn't captured his entry from orbit, but anyone skilled in reading surveillance images—including the weather AI, if it was programmed to look—would recognize the landing furrow.

The interesting data came from the settlement company. His query had inadvertently exploited a security weakness and garnered him the company's backup hypercube of corporate data and correspondence. A younger version of himself might've hesitated to read it, but being made into a research project had scoured the shine off his idealism.

He woke Bethnee. She sat up and pushed her hair back from her face. "What time is it?"

"Zero six hundred. Sorry, but we need to talk." He

pointed to the table, where he'd set out a pitcher of water, cups, and two mealpacks. "Breakfast."

She stood and stretched again, and he looked away. The one glimpse of her mid-thigh-length sleeping tunic that clung to her high breasts, flared hips, and flat stomach threatened to derail his rational thoughts. He waited until he heard her moving, then turned back to watch her limp toward the fresher door because she drew him like a magnet. She was definitely walking more easily than before.

When she returned, she looked more alert. "My leg is feeling good. Want to scan it?"

"Later. Are you awake enough to think deep thoughts?"

She sat. "Depends on the subject. I can't solve the time-versus-distance paradox in interstellar transit physics before breakfast." She triggered the mealpack's heater.

He laughed as he sat and triggered his own. "I'll tell the Concordance Science Achievement Award Committee to stand down, then."

She pointed to the display he'd left for her on the table. "What's this?"

"Background reading." He reached across the table to turn it on. "It's why the wakeup call."

She nodded, then took a bite and started reading the highlights he'd hastily put together. He saw on her face the moment she got to the part that had caused him to wake her so early.

"Holy hells. We have to warn the town. Daylight is only five hours from now." She stabbed her fork toward the display. "And what the hell kind of audit takes a team of eleven to conduct one for a town of a hundred?"

"This is going to sound paranoid, but I think the audit is a cover for something else. A raid, a theft..."

Bethnee's eyes widened. "A hunt for a CPS fugitive." She stood abruptly. "You can't stay here."

He shook his head. "I have to." He crossed his arms. "It could be legit. The settlement company might be making a zero-tolerance example of Tanimai for cheating. If I get caught, the company could fine the town hard credits for not detaining and reporting an unregistered settler. If I'm the target, I don't want CPS hunters anywhere near the town. I won't go back willingly, and they wouldn't care about collateral damage. Which is why I want you to take the animals to the safety of your cave."

She stared at him for a long moment, and he braced himself for an argument. Her expression of fear and worry morphed into resignation. "Okay." She shoved her hands in her pockets. "You know what you can and can't do. I hate leaving you here alone, but I'm worthless in a fight, and I don't want the animals to be casualties, or hostages for your cooperation."

He let out the breath he didn't realized he'd been holding. "Thank you." Her trust humbled him. He resolved to be worthy of it.

BETHNEE MADE it look easy to load a menagerie of animals into the close confines of the flitter. He'd probably still be trying to catch one of the cats.

He handed Bethnee an earwire. "A spare for our private net."

She put it in the top pocket of her coat. "Okay."

He handed her a slender length of rounded incalloy, with padding at one end and a bulge of fine wire net at the other. "Homemade shockstick." He showed her how to operate it. "It's Nuñez's Solstice Day gift, because that asshole at the spaceport transfer dock confiscated hers."

Bethnee nodded. "It's a great gift, and she'll love it. Thank you."

He handed her a small, flat box tied with a tiny strand of fiber cable, looped in a bow. "Your Solstice Day gift. Open it when you're safe."

She rewarded him with a shy smile as she slid it into her lower pocket. "I'll ping you when I get home."

He fought a strong urge to fold her into an embrace, because her departure felt too much like goodbye. He stiffened his spine and stepped back.

She opened the flitter's pilot-side door, then hesitated and turned back. "Do you think I'm still warped by the recovery chems?"

"I doubt it. They usually metabolize in six or eight hours, tops."

"Okay." She stepped up and in, then turned to face him. "Then I think you should know, I still want to kiss you. Be safe, Axur Tragon."

She closed the door and lifted off ninety seconds later, by his internal chrono.

He buried his roiling emotions under the activities of dowsing the glow lights and resetting the various analog security measures as he went back to his house. He prayed to the constant stars that the audit was just an audit, and that he'd be seeing Bethnee again soon, because he sure as hell wanted to be kissed by her, and return the favor.

10

Bethnee sent a short message from the air to Nuñez, but she had her hands full with flying and keeping threads of talent on eleven animals. Twice she nearly turned around when she remembered the look of longing on Axur's face when she'd impulsively told him she wanted to kiss him.

She pinged him the moment after she got the animals settled in the cave, and put out fresh water and food. Nuñez pinged a moment later. Bethnee told her what Axur had said about the audit timed for sunrise, and his suspicion about a hidden agenda.

"Farking settlement company assholes," Nuñez said vehemently. *"I'll get the local comm net going, in case the settlement company is monitoring the uplink, too."*

"I'll return your flitter to the clinic, and go home on my glide board."

"Okay. I'll open the gate for the yaks."

Bethnee disconnected, then took a minute to send images to Axur's animals so they'd know the cave's layout and how to operate the pet doors. She wanted them to always have an escape route.

She grabbed her glide board, set the security system, and walked as fast as she could to the flitter, feeling time slipping away. It wasn't until after she was in the air that she realized she'd limped very little on the snowy path.

AFTER DELIVERING the flitter and Nuñez's present, Bethnee rode her board out of town. Just as she passed the last building, Nuñez pinged. Bethnee started to answer, but her friend was already talking.

"...he won't hurt you if you stay still. What are you two doing in my paddock? Back up, Upolu." Upolu was a large yak bull, with wickedly curled, sharp horns and a dislike for strangers. Nuñez's conversation continued after a moment. *"Well, there's nothing to see back here but yak shit. I'll need to see your IDs and verify them with settlement compa–"*

The connection cut off.

Everyone in Tanimai knew about the yaks and the geese, so the interlopers had to be the auditors, come early. The "inadvertent" comm was Nuñez's way of warning her. Bethnee grounded the glide board and sent a quick warning to Nuñez's spouse, then pinged Axur with the news.

"Where are you?"

"Edge of town. I'm–" An ear-splitting, chest-rumbling

whump made her instinctively duck her head like a turtle. "I just heard a crash, but I can't see anything. I'll check the animals in the area." She sent threads of her talent out to all the animals she could find, both domestic and wild, and took advantage of their superior hearing and night vision to glean information. "I think it came from the Administrative Center. The building is collapsed inward."

"Isn't that where the satellite uplink is? Check your local comms."

She tried her percomp and the extra comm bracelet. "They're down."

"The best thing you can do is go home."

"I can't leave Nuñez."

"She has thick walls and neighbors and attack geese. You're alone on a glide board. You're brave as hell, and I can't tell you what to do, but I will tell you that the hardest lesson a Jumper learns is when to retreat."

She blew out a frustrated breath. He was right. "Okay, here's my offer. I'll go home, if you'll use your fancy tech to figure out what's going on, and get help for Nuñez and the town if needed."

"Deal. Stay safe, Bethnee Bakonin."

She launched into the air again and hunkered down behind the board's wedge front to reduce wind drag. Guilt gave her second, third, and tenth thoughts about her decision. It felt like she was abandoning the truly good and generous woman who had saved her life and helped her learn how to live on her own. Bethnee would never forgive herself if Nuñez got hurt, but she'd also never forgive herself if she became the lever to bend Nuñez to their will.

11
_____

Bethnee was so distracted with visions of calamity that she almost didn't notice the first sign that someone had breached her perimeter. The gossamer lengths of fiberet cable trailed down to the ground instead of invisibly spanning between the trees. An air vehicle had flown through and broken them, triggering the chemical reaction that made them faintly glow.

She veered off north into the trees and turned off the board's light, flying by terrain sensors alone. She slowed to almost a hover, a meter above the forest floor, maneuvering around the trees and boulders.

She heard voices. A man and a woman.

"What the hell is this sticky stuff?" The man sounded outraged.

"Move slow. Grab my hand." The woman sounded like she was suppressing laughter.

Bethnee grounded her board quietly behind a tree and

buried it in the snow, fighting hard against instincts compelling her to run. The animals needed her to stay.

She sent threads of her talent to her animals and Axur's to tell them all to hide in the caves.

She heard squelching sounds as the intruder walked through her moat that had a mix of yak dung, mineral salts, and scrap glass road glue, kept warm by a geothermally heated grid at the bottom. Once he got out, cold air would turn the thick coating on his clothes glass-hard.

Bethnee took a deep breath and let it out slowly, then peeked around the tree trunk. Two figures in one-piece blue snowsuits and transparent snow hoods trudged through the snow, away from the moat. The taller figure scraped the orange gunk off his butt as he walked. She opened her talent senses, but as usual, the humans felt like ghosts. She extended further and felt two more ghosts, clustered near the front of her cabin. That was more than a third of the auditor team.

She limped as fast as she dared to the edge of the trees. The interlopers were using both flying and hand lights. They'd see her if she tried crossing the main path.

She coaxed a nearby wild owl into looking at the front yard and borrowed the owl's superb hearing. Three men and a woman, all in one-piece snowsuits, stood at her front door.

"...haven't got all day," the woman groused. "Let's get the power-ram to breach that door and look, then get the hell out of here. I don't like being restricted to stunners and tranqs." She sounded irritated.

"That's 'cause you'll shoot anything that moves." A wide-shouldered man opened a display.

The man who'd been in the moat looked down as he stomped his legs. "Fucking mud is freezing, even through my suit."

"Like you're any better," snapped the woman. She pointed to the display. "What does the tech scanner say?"

"House has powered security, but nothing outside... No, wait. One double-tech signature. That way, and close." The owl's vision showed her an image of a man pointing into the woods.

Ice flooded Bethnee's veins as she frantically powered down her earwire and comms bracelet, berating herself for stupidity.

"Signal died." He tapped the display on the heel of his hand a couple of times.

The woman focused on the main path. "If it's the vet, she can just let us in. Keeps us on schedule."

They must have figured out where she lived from homestead records. They hadn't asked permission to land, but it didn't pay to piss off auditors, if that's what they were. Especially auditors with weapons.

Her only hope was to lure them into the woods and into her various security measures. None of them were fatal, just strong deterrents for the uninvited. She switched her battery-powered wrist light to low-power green and risked brief flashes to tell her where to step over rocks and duck under the branches. Learning every meter of her property in light and dark had helped her feel safe. She skirted around the fifteen-meter clearing. On the far side, she switched her comms bracelet on and off, mimicking an intermittent signal.

Two interlopers came through the trees, their lights marking their progress. She backed further into the shadows. They plunged into the virgin snow of the clearing. A faint whipping sound whistled in the air.

"Son of a bitch!"

"Who the hell leaves coiled spikewire in the middle of farking nowhere?"

Bethnee took advantage of their noise to make her way down the hill. An empty flitter occupied her gravel landing pad. She limped behind it and down into trees and rocks to the southeast. Adrenaline jacked up her tension and turned her stomach sour. Her thigh spasmed.

The sound of another approaching flitter echoed against the mountainside.

She scrambled under nearby shrubs and let the disturbed snow cover her. A smaller flitter landed behind the first. Two people exited and walked toward her house.

"...enforcers are coming to investigate." A woman's voice with a Mandarin accent. "Trummler wants us out by local dawn."

"I thought the auditor was supposed to intercept any calls from the area. We paid her enough." A man's voice, muffled by a high collar.

"Call came from an ex-Jumper, so the dispatcher took it seriously." The woman didn't sound happy.

Bethnee would have smiled if she weren't so scared. Clever Axur had found help.

Their words confirmed they weren't auditors, which meant they were after something or someone else. She didn't know what to do besides distract them so they'd leave her house alone, and delay them long enough so they'd run out of time and leave.

She'd never imagined she'd be wishing for a speedy visit by the Del'Arche Planetary Enforcers.

BETHNEE HAD CRAMMED herself into a rock hollow, wracking her brain for ideas. She was exhausted, and out of options, because dawn was coming.

The intruders failed to breach her house's physical and tech security, and had grown increasingly irritated about not catching her. Especially after two of them fell down a steep hill and the others had to deploy ropes to help them up the loose debris underfoot. They'd grown more wary of her traps after that.

She reached out once again to the animals to make sure they were safe. To her dismay, she discovered Trouble, the e-dog, was outside the cave and headed toward her. His fleeting thoughts listened to the controller in his head with Axur's order to find Bethnee and protect her. She refused to put any of the animals in jeopardy for her.

"Got her!" said a male voice. "It's faint, but the scanner says she's twenty-three meters south, and moving closer. I'll send lights."

Trouble's controller was permanently on, meaning the intruders were keying on him. She'd promised Axur she'd keep his animals safe.

With trembling fingers, she powered on both her higher-powered comms bracelets and her earwire, then pinged Axur. She subvocalized as she slid out of the hollow and stood. "I hope you hear this soon. Six people are at my place. They can't get into my house. They've been chasing me. I'm going to let them catch me, or they'll hurt Trouble. Send the enforcers here if you can."

She limped her way out from under the trees. She didn't have to go far before lights flew close and a black-haired man and a blonde woman, both with blood spots on their pant legs, came toward her at a fast walk. She turned and ran away, exaggerating her limp so it looked like her top speed.

"Get her!" shouted the man.

The blonde woman ran, then launched herself at Bethnee to take them both tumbling down into the snow. The blonde woman rose to her knees and roughly pulled off Bethnee's comm bracelets and earwire and threw them away. "You won't be needing these." She grinned like a shark. "I heard something bad happened to the town's satellite uplink." She grabbed Bethnee's arm and hauled her to her feet, then jabbed Bethnee's shoulder with an unpowered shockstick. "Where is it? Where's the shipment?"

"Wait," said the black-haired man. "The boss will want to hear this. Bring her to the cabin." He tilted his head toward her house.

The woman clamped a strong hand on Bethnee's arm and pulled her along. Bethnee limped as slowly as she dared, using the time trudging through the thigh-high snow to touch the strong, trusting minds of her animal family to keep herself from falling into a fog of fear. Her thigh muscle cramped once, then quieted. A small victory.

Three more people stood near her front door, all wearing the same new-looking blue snowsuits. They must have sent the man with the ruined one back to the flitter to stay warm. An Asian woman stood and watched, arms crossed and fingers drumming, as a dark-skinned man with an upright crest of flame-red hair folded and pocketed a scanner. The third, a noticeably shorter man, pulled down his collar and stepped closer. He stared at her legs, then looked intently at her face. "Well, well, the God of the Gaps has finally answered my prayers. It's Indenturee Bakonin."

She knew that face and voice from her worst nightmares. Kanaway, the guard with chems and perversions. The pieces fell into place. They weren't a freelance theft crew raiding the town, or CPS operatives looking for Axur. They were mercenaries after the bounty for a lost shipment of valuable designer pets. The shaking started, and coherent thought began to disintegrate. She desperately sent her talent out to every animal she could reach with the imperative to stay hidden. She forced herself to focus on the Asian woman's combat boots, counting toe taps. The animals depended on her to buy time for whoever was responding to Axur's call for help.

"What's wrong with her?" asked the black-haired man.

Kanaway grinned. "Oh, the little subbin' bitch wants me so bad she's trembling. Did you miss me?"

She shuddered, but somehow found the courage to look at him straight in the eye. "I hope Breitenbahn liked the record of what you did." She glanced down at his crotch. "Cured your soft and tiny problem yet?"

The blonde woman guffawed loud and long.

Rage flared in Kanaway's eyes as he slapped Bethnee. "That fake vid got me blacklisted from the trade." He slapped her again, harder. She staggered with the impact. She straightened up and watched him warily. At least her time in Breitenbahn's cruel circus had taught her how to take a hit.

The Asian woman gave Kanaway a hard look. "Enough." She turned and gave Bethnee a plastic smile. "We're looking for a pet-trade shipment." Her tone turned cajoling. "Help us, and we'll give you a percentage of the reward."

Bethnee spat blood on the snowy ground near Kanaway's boots and said nothing.

The Asian woman sighed and gestured toward the man with the red mohawk. "Domaki, find out where the shipment is and let's go." She cast an annoyed look at Kanaway. "Move, Kanaway."

Kanaway's thin lips curled in hatred, but he stepped back. In Bethnee's jagged memories, he was big and impossibly strong, but seeing him now made her realize he was actually shorter than her.

The red-haired man moved closer. "She's hard to read." He took off his glove. "I need to touch her."

The blonde woman grabbed Bethnee's arm, stripped off her glove, and forced her to hold out her hand. Domaki grabbed Bethnee's trembling, ice-cold fingers.

Bethnee felt the man's telepathic talent questing for her mind and memories. She plunged her mind into Jynx's and focused on the snow leopard's alien thoughts.

Distantly, she heard words with her ears and in her

mind, but Bethnee-the-leopard ignored them as unimportant.

Domaki pushed a succession of images of pet-trade animals at her. She didn't recognize any of them until he got to a foo dog and six-legged chimera with two tails. She pulled out of Jynx's mind, because snow leopards didn't know how to lie. Bethnee shot Domaki a memory of when she'd treated Kivo for the near-fatal illness and his breathing had stopped. *Dead.*

All of them? demanded Domaki.

She felt him nibbling away at the corners of her mind, trying to access other memories. She called up image after image of animals she'd raised on Breitenbahn's ship, and let Domaki feel her deep sadness for each one she'd lost.

How do you know Kanaway?

The question took her by surprise, leaving her vulnerable to Domaki's probe into her darker memories. When he touched the worst of them, she felt the first wave of the familiar deep, seizure-like tremors.

Frelling hell! Domaki apparently didn't like her memories any more than she did.

She spitefully sent him the indelible image of how she'd looked after Kanaway finished, with a swollen face, and bruises and blood everywhere. How he'd shoved her half-conscious naked body into a ship's autodoc to heal away evidence of the assault, unaware that the ship's security monitors recorded his actions.

Domaki hastily withdrew from Bethnee's mind. She collapsed to her knees, heart racing, gasping for breath, unable to control her shudders.

Domaki backed away. "The research chimera died some time back. She hasn't seen any of the other animals."

"Bullshit," snarled Kanaway. His hands curled into fists. "She's the only small-animal vet on the planet. She's a stubborn, lying bitch."

Domaki gave Kanaway a disgusted look. "Don't tell me how to do my job, you warped little twist." Domaki pulled on his glove. "It's been eleven months since the bounty was posted for that shipment, and the active tracers are in a herd of mountain goats, not high-end pets. She doesn't know anything." He looked to the orange-tinged horizon. "If we leave now, we can meet Blue team at Point Exeter before it gets light."

"She'll have animals in her house." Kanaway could sound very reasonable when he wanted to. "If any of them are valuable, we can at least show a profit."

Domaki shoved his hands under his armpits and shook his head. "Ain't gonna be me that compels her to let us in." He cast another disgusted look at Kanaway. "Too many bad memories."

"Give me five minutes with her," said Kanaway, his tone persuasive. "I bet I can get her to talk."

The Asian woman hesitated, then shook her head. "No more fishing. We're out of time. Trummler okayed this mission because Kanaway's intel pointed to Del'Arche for where the high-value shipment ended up, and it'd be a quick in-and-out to question the only two veterinarians. This is a bust." She waved a hand to encompass everyone. "Flitters airborne in five. Let's go." She pointed to Domaki. "Ride with Kanaway."

With the Asian woman leading, they walked

purposefully down the path toward the flitters. Bethnee pivoted on her knees to watch them go. She tried to follow them with her talent, but it was like trying to follow phantoms.

She waited until the last of them vanished up the path, then sent her talent out to search for Trouble. He was appallingly close, under a tree, and would have been an easy target if one of the mercs had seen him. She collapsed onto her heels and let the muddy yellow dog come to her, even though it wouldn't be truly safe until the flitters took off.

Trouble allowed her to put an arm around him and hug him close. She wished the blonde woman hadn't stripped her Axur-net earwire, so she could hear his voice again.

Inexplicably, Trouble pulled away and stared intently at the path, growling softly.

"Come on, Domaki." Kanaway's voice. "The sooner we find my pet-tracer scanner, the sooner we get off this ice ball."

Bethnee sent a panicked imperative to Trouble to run, but it was too late. Kanaway and Domaki strode into view, their flying lights illuminating her and Trouble.

Kanaway looked triumphant. "This really is my lucky day." He pulled a stunner out of his pocket and casually shot Domaki twice. Domaki's body jolted like he'd been struck by lightning, then crumpled.

Kanaway aimed the stunner at her. "You're worth ten times the bounty of that old research shipment." Avarice lit his face. "And I know just the buyer. He's been looking for you for three years."

12

* GDAT 3241.265 *

Axur landed the runabout on the flat rocks above Bethnee's cave just as the sun crept over the mountaintops, burnishing their white tops with gold. She'd pointed out the path the first day he'd been there to meet Jynx. He loaded his gear and started down the steep trail. He sped up when he overheard one of the mercs say he'd forgotten a scanner and would catch up to the others soon. Merc companies weren't usually that disorganized.

Bethnee was likely paying the price for his mistakes, not the least of which was forgetting that the experimental tech in his cybernetics wasn't the only thing of value in the frozen north. He'd already been loading his runabout when he'd received her ping that she was planning to protect Trouble by letting the mercs catch her. He should have taken into account her willingness to sacrifice herself to protect the animals she loved. Her pet-trade captors had taught her she had no value, and he hadn't found the right time or words to tell her how much she meant to him.

At least the Del'Arche Planetary Enforcers were on their way. He'd lucked into an ex-Jumper answering his ping, and she'd believed him and agreed to send help. Then he'd used his experimental tech to crack the raiders' temporary comms net.

They were a mercenary company specializing in freelance bounty hunts. While a southern squad went after a trio of brothers whose capture would bring a big payday back in the Concordance, a smaller northern squad went north for a stolen shipment of designer pets with a high reward, and anything else they could steal while they were at it. They considered a small frontier town as easy reaping.

They'd only intended to disable the town's satellite uplink, but the cheaply made building had collapsed. The three culprits had joined their two teammates at Nuñez's vet clinic, where they'd been attacked by pissed-off geese and nearly been gored by an enraged yak. That team beat a hasty retreat to rendezvous with the main squad to the south. The remaining six went after veterinarian Bethnee because they knew the coordinates of her homestead.

The same homestead to which he, like the flatliner he was, had sent her and his animals, thinking to keep them out of harm's way. He was only slightly relieved when the merc company's few comms after that told him they weren't finding her to be easy reaping, either.

From the trees near her cabin, he heard a man's voice but couldn't make out the words, and he couldn't tell where it was coming from. He wished he had hearing like a dog's... but he did, sort of. He quickly tuned his experimental tech to Trouble's command processor, and pulled the auditory feeds.

"...the door right now, your filthy dog dies in front of you." A man's baritone but nasal voice, full of menace. *"And you know I'll do it, too."*

"It's open." Bethnee's ordinarily expressive voice sounded flat and defeated. Axur clenched his jaw.

"You first. No surprises."

Axur crept closer.

"Are you going to leave Domaki down on the path? He'll freeze." Her tone said she didn't care if he did.

"That's his problem. Slimy, subbin' minder. He was going to tell Na Ming lies about me, just like you did with that fake surveillance vid you sent Breitenbahn. He blamed me for your escape."

Axur eased westward, close enough to see a red-haired man down, blocking the path to the flitter pad. He quickly stripped the unconscious man's weapons, percomp, and earwire, then zip-tied his wrists and ankles and rolled him off the path into the ditch full of snow. The heated snowsuit would protect him from the cold for a while.

"Turn on the lights," said the man with Bethnee and Trouble. *"Where are the other animals?"*

Axur ran down the path to the flitter, which they'd obligingly left unlocked. He pried open the control panel and used his homemade high-powered shockstick to good effect.

"I only have one other. This house is too small for him.

Axur mostly lives in his den up the mountain, but he's closer today."

Axur smiled and let relief take some of his tension as he exited the flitter. Bethnee knew he was there, and was buying time. He sobered quickly, because she was playing a dangerous game.

"Pet trade?"

Axur ran up the path toward Bethnee's house.

"No."

"Liar. Make him come to you."

Axur used his cybernetic strength to jump to the top of the big three-meter-high rock in Bethnee's front yard, which made him less immediately noticeable if her captor happened to look outside. The sun was already over the trees, and would soon be curving higher.

"I can't get around his controller. He's not pet trade, he's a military-enhanced experimental."

Axur heard the unmistakable sound of a slap.

"Call him, or I'll stun the dog and you both. Maybe have some naked playtime with you. Find out if you still like it rough and dirty."

Axur unslung his flechette gun and extended the guide for distance shots. His freighter had been sadly lacking in powered beamers, blasters, or railguns, so he'd made some analog weapons of his own, and practiced with them.

The mercenary comms band flared to life in his ear with an abrupt tone. *"Kanaway, Domaki, what's the holdup?"* The Mandarin-accented voice of the team leader sounded exasperated.

"Uh, Domaki tripped on something in the vet's yard

and got stunned. I'm rigging something to carry him on." Axur rolled his eyes at Kanaway's unbelievably thin story.

"Quit fucking around, Kanaway, or I'll term you." The team leader disconnected without waiting for Kanaway's reply.

Kanaway's ugly laugh rang out. *"Stupid pig doesn't know what and who you are. I'll take you by myself, and make Breitenbahn bleed mega credits to get you back. His business isn't so good since you left."*

Axur found a quasi-prone position on the rock and aimed his gun with its homemade flechettes loaded with quick-acting dormo. All he needed was a clear shot at Kanaway's bare skin.

"Call the animal. Now."

"We have to go outside, and leave the dog in here, or Axur won't come at all."

"Bullshit."

"Shoot me, then. Good luck carrying me all the way to your flitter and taking off before your crew comes looking. No grav carts around here like on Breitenbahn's ship."

Stunner fire sounded, and Trouble yelped loudly in pain. Axur forced himself to let it roll off him, or he wouldn't be calm enough to make the shot.

"Outside!"

After a long, tense moment, Bethnee limped slowly through the doorway, then stumbled forward when the man shoved her. "Call him!"

She winced with every step as she limped haltingly toward the center of the little yard and stopped. Kanaway followed too close to her for Axur to shoot him. She bowed her head for a long moment, then turned to her right and looked expectantly toward the trees.

Kanaway clamped one cruel hand on her neck and with his other, pointed the stunner toward the trees. A large raven landed in the tree and screeched loudly, making Kanaway twitch.

A flicker of movement on Axur's right tugged at his attention. He risked a quick glance and caught a glimpse of a large, black-furred shadow stalking through the snow.

Axur winced at the loud tone in his merc comms earwire.

"Kanaway, we're coming for you and Domaki. Trummler's order." The team leader sounded disgruntled.

Kanaway let go of Bethnee's neck just long enough to touch his own earwire. "I'm already in the air." He spoke aloud rather than subvocalizing.

"Your flitter's tracer is reporting itself as damaged and stolen. We'll meet you in Tanimai."

Kanaway swore but said he'd be there, then touched the earwire. He stomped his foot in frustration and grabbed Bethnee's neck again and forcibly turned her toward the path. "Let's go."

She took one step, then stumbled sideways and landed on one knee. Kanaway let go as he struggled to keep his balance.

A black blur shot out from the trees to the west. Kanaway saw the movement, but too late to avoid being knocked down by a determined dire wolf. Kanaway's stunner sailed into the air and landed on the snowy gravel.

The man rolled sideways and up to his hands and knees. He crawled fast toward the fallen weapon, but had to duck and cover his face to avoid the attack of a huge black raven, cawing noisily, diving straight for him with talons outstretched. He threw himself toward the stunner, but not in time to stop the other black raven from stealing it in a flurry of flight.

Axur kept his gun trained on Kanaway, but couldn't get a clear angle without shooting Serena, who stood between Kanaway and Bethnee, shoulder fur fluffed stiff, growling menacingly.

Kanaway scrambled to his feet and spun to face the new threat. He held a phase knife in the stance of an experienced fighter. He touched his earwire and spoke aloud instead of subvocalizing. "Hey, Na Ming. Bring the big flitter back to the vet's house and get the tranq guns ready. She's got a fortune in stolen pets, starting with a trained dire wolf."

After a long moment, the Mandarin-accented woman's voice answered. *"Okay, but you better be on the level."* Na Ming sounded supremely testy. *"We're fifteen minutes out."*

"See you soon." Kanaway touched his earwire again. His eyes hadn't once left the wolf. "Company's coming. Give us the pets, or I'll tell them what you are and what you're worth."

Bethnee stayed on her knees and said nothing.

Kanaway sidestepped toward the open door of Bethnee's house. "Since you were so anxious to get me out of your house, the others must be in there."

Axur wished he could talk to Bethnee, but since he couldn't, he reviewed his mission parameters. Protecting her was top priority, but she now had reinforcements from his animals, and probably hers. His secondary objective called for protecting them all from the mercenaries, which was a better use of his skills and resources, but it meant he'd have to leave Bethnee with a monster.

Axur fucking hated the hard choices of war.

13

Bethnee felt like she was floating. Adrenaline still soured her stomach and made her shake, but she'd apparently hit her limit on fear, and had no more to give.

Kanaway sneered. "Hey, Bakonin. How much does a dire wolf bring at auction?"

The man was trying to keep her afraid, not thinking. She'd had enough of that to last a lifetime. "I don't know. How much do you think I can trade for Domaki?" She'd seen through the raven's eyes when Axur had pushed the telepath into the snowdrift. "Wonder what he'll tell your bosses?"

Kanaway huffed. "They won't believe him. They know minders are all liars."

She sent a thread of talent to cue preciously cute, plump Shiza, the little foo dog with the fierce heart of a lion. He waddled out into the weak midday sun and barked.

Kanaway turned. A slow, greedy smile formed. "See? Liars."

She asked Shiza to step closer to the man, but stay out of his reach. "Don't pick him up," she warned.

"What's he going to do, drool on me?" Kanaway laughed derisively.

Bethnee took a nervous breath, then sent Shiza instructions. He barked once, then turned to go back inside the house.

Kanaway glanced at the dire wolf, then focused on the foo dog. "Come here, you expensive little shit." His tone was baby-talk sweet as he patted his thigh.

Shiza slowed and turned to look up. Lightning fast, Kanaway dropped his phase knife to grab Shiza by the curly mane with both hands and drag him closer.

Enraged, Shiza twisted and bit down on Kanaway's exposed wrist.

Kanaway screamed and shook his arm, then rocked back a step back and kicked Shiza's ribs. The foo dog didn't let go. If Kanaway noticed a white weasel dart in and steal the phase knife, it didn't register.

Kanaway dropped to his knees, yelling, trying to roll Shiza onto his side. The foo dog planted his feet and used his strong neck and broad shoulder muscles to stay upright.

Bethnee climbed unsteadily to her feet and moved to stand by Serena.

"Get it off me!" He punched the dog's head, which caused Shiza to clamp down again even harder.

"Shiza," said Bethnee. She used her talent to help the foo dog realize he'd won. Shiza gave the man's crushed, bloody arm a tearing shake, then opened his wide, square jaws and scrabbled backward.

Kanaway lifted his good hand toward his face, but froze when Shiza keened and bared his sharp, bloody teeth.

Bethnee realized he'd been reaching for his earwire. She couldn't let him call for help. Before she could talk herself out of it, she pivoted in and stripped it off his face, then pivoted back. Her torn fingernail left a welt along his jaw. Blood welled immediately.

He swung a slow, sloppy punch at her. His venomous look would have once quelled her. He lifted his knee to put one foot on the ground. "You're fucking dead."

"No, but you are." She invited Shiza to come closer to her. The little dog limped a little as he moved to lean against her knee. "Foo dog poison is neuro-hemorrhagic, designed to kill quick, and you got two full injections. I told you not to pick him up."

"Bullshi'..." He shook his head as if trying to clear it. "They're sold to children... Prob'ly fast dormo or somethin'." His words slurred as he absently wiped red-stained drool off his chin with his good hand. The injured arm drooped listlessly at his side, gushing a pool of bright red blood onto the snow-whitened gravel. "You're gonn' be my ticket back..."

He slumped forward over his knee, then toppled sideways. He shuddered, then lay still.

Bethnee thought she should have felt something, watching the horror of her nightmares draw his last two wet, gurgling breaths, but nothing came. She had no more time to worry about it. Four greedy mercenaries with tranq guns were about to land on her doorstep.

She sent her talent out to check on the animals, but she was on her last reserves. Coordinating dire wolves, ravens, weasels, and foo dogs to defeat Kanaway had been like running a marathon. She asked bruised Shiza to go inside to protect injured, still dazed Trouble.

She wished she were a telepath like Domaki, so she could communicate with Axur, instead of just sensing his general location. She absently shoved the earwire she'd stripped from Kanaway into her chest pocket, only to find the one Axur had given her already there. Kicking herself for forgetting, she put it on and subvocalized a message. "Kanaway is dead in my front yard. I'm resetting the cabin's security. Tell me what I can do."

He came online almost immediately. *"Are you okay? Are you hurt? I've moved some of your traps to arrange welcome surprises for the mercs. They're running late. With luck, the enforcers will catch them here."*

She hadn't realized how much she'd needed to hear the sound of his voice until that moment.

"Tired. A bruise or two. Shiza and Trouble need treatment."

"I don't suppose you'd go back inside the cave and stay there?"

"Not a chance. It's my farking homestead. Can Serena and I come down the path?"

"Yes, I'll meet you. It's going to get crowded around here soon, and I want us all to be ready when it does."

14

* GDAT 3241.265 *

Axur hung up his poncho, then sat with Bethnee on the small couch in her chilly cabin and watched the two planetary enforcers standing near the front door. Their orders were to keep an eye him and Bethnee, but they were more interested in friendly Kivo.

The other enforcers who'd landed took custody of the mercs. With Bethnee and the animals acting as lookout, Axur had lured the mercs into Bethnee's traps, then shot them with one of their own tranq guns. Because one merc was dead, the enforcers insisted on waiting for their commander to arrive with Pranteaux, the Tanimai town administrator.

Axur stole glances at Bethnee. She looked bruised, tired, and pale, but not flatlined. He admired the hell out of her.

Shiza the foo dog now sat across her lap and partly into his, contentedly drooling a wet spot on both their pant legs. Bethnee finger-combed his curly mane. She surprised Axur by sliding her hand into his and mouthing the words "thank you." He squeezed her hand gently in acknowledgment.

A few minutes later, a tall, muscular woman in uniform and flexin armor, and a short, rotund man in a puffy-collared, plaid long coat entered the cabin.

The short man blinked and squinted as he looked around with disdain. His eyes widened when he saw Kivo, then narrowed when his gaze landed on Bethnee and Axur. He drew breath to speak, but the woman beat him to it.

"I'm Commander Cherkogin, and I'm sure you know Administrator Pranteaux." She took in her surroundings with darting glances, then focused on Axur. "Tragon?"

"Yes, sir." He stifled the urge to salute.

Cherkogin turned her gaze to Bethnee. "You must be Vetmed Bakonin."

Pranteaux cleared his throat loudly. "She's the landed homesteader." He made it sound like an infectious disease. "I'll bet he's the illegal settler who's been trading in town." He pointed a curling, accusing finger at Axur.

Cherkogin frowned. "First things first, Administrator." She tilted her head toward Bethnee's front yard. "How did the merc die?"

"Foo dog poison," said Bethnee, patting Shiza's shoulder. She explained the events in terse sentences. By the time she was done, Pranteaux was staring at the sleepy foo dog in horror.

Cherkogin looked at Axur. "We intercepted the rest of the merc company where you said they'd be." She hooked her thumbs in her utility belt. "The DPE takes a dim view of kidnapping Del'Arche settlers or stealing from homesteaders." She turned to Pranteaux with a sly smile. "And an equally dim view of destroying valuable protection animals like foo dogs."

Pranteaux's mouth gaped like a fish. "But it *killed* a man!" He looked back and forth between the foo dog and Cherkogin's unyielding expression. He blew out a frustrated breath, then glared at Bethnee and pointed at Axur again. "He's still illegal. He's been skulking around for months. I've been trying to catch him."

A fleeting look of distaste crossed Cherkogin's face as she turned away from Pranteaux to meet Axur's gaze. "What's your status?"

Axur had known this moment was inevitable ever since he'd chosen to meet the enforcers, so he could be there to protect Bethnee when they questioned her. He let go of her hand so he could stand, but she held him fast.

"He's my plus one."

Axur hoped he kept his confusion off his face. Cherkogin raised an eyebrow.

Pranteaux gawped, then recovered. "He can't be. You're not a paid settler. You can't tell me he lives in this pile of logs with you." His mouth twisted in disdain as he looked her up and down. "You hate men."

"I don't hate men." Bethnee let go of Axur's hand, then gently urged Shiza to jump down and got to her feet. "I'm afraid of men who want to hurt me. There's a difference."

Axur stood and stayed next to her. Whatever her play was, he was in.

Bethnee pushed her hair behind her ear. "I looked it up. The settlement contract says homesteaders get one 'plus one,' as long as he agrees to reside on my homestead for a GDAT standard year." Bethnee wove her fingers through his and held up their joined hands. "I'm declaring Axur as my plus one."

Cherkogin smiled. "I'll be your official witness." She raised her arm to tap her percomp gauntlet. Her smile turned sharper. "I'll even register the declaration for you, since the town's satellite uplink building got destroyed by the greedy mercs that your 'plus one' helped stop." She directed her next words to Pranteaux with a pointed look. "He single-handedly saved your town from an armed invasion and wholesale theft of its valuable animals."

Axur tilted his head toward Bethnee. "She delayed this team so you could catch them."

Pranteaux clamped his jaw and looked away with a frown. His eyes widened, and his expression morphed into sly challenge. "Clause 624.308.T.51." He looked at Bethnee. "You'll have to cohab or marry your 'plus one.'" He gave Axur an insulting smile. "Can't have Slick Slims taking advantage of the gullible and stealing their homesteads." He looked around at the furniture and sneered. "Not that this dump is worth stealing."

Cherkogin shook her head. "The council rescinded that stupid clause two years ago. You can't force people into domestic contracts."

Pranteaux jutted out his jaw, clearly intending to continue the fight.

Cherkogin was having none of it. "Quarks and quasars, man, I brought you here to confirm Bakonin's identity as the homesteader and remand the mercs if needed, not meddle in people's private lives." She shot quick glances to her patiently waiting enforcers. "The administrator's work here is done. Escort him back to the flitter."

Pranteaux gave everyone in the room one last, sweeping glare and stomped through the door that commander had already opened. The enforcers left with him.

"Bureaucrats," muttered Cherkogin. She kept the door open and turned to Bethnee. "Would you mind stepping outside and, uh, getting your dire wolf guardian to stand down?"

Bethnee snorted. "You could have just said you want to talk to Axur alone." She sealed the coat she hadn't yet taken off and limped to the door. She left without a backward glance. The door closed behind her.

"Sorry," said Cherkogin, with a shrug. "I tank at diplomacy."

"Apologize to her, not me." He tilted his head, finally able to place her familiar-sounding voice. "You were the ex-Jumper dispatcher this morning."

She nodded. "Yep. We're really short-handed. How'd you like a job with the Del'Arche Planetary Enforcers?"

BETHNEE'S HEAD pounded and her joints ached from the fever she'd brought on herself by healing both Trouble and Shiza. Her talent felt thin and wispy as she extended a thread of invitation to Serena, who was sitting in the middle of her front yard, keeping herself between Bethnee and the waiting enforcers. Serena stood and trotted toward her.

Snapping at the commander hadn't been her finest moment. She heard Cherkogin's job offer right as the door closed. It was ideal for Axur. He'd have purpose again and make new friends, because Axur was very likeable. He'd have a team of enforcers to protect him if the CPS ever came calling.

Bethnee sat on a flat rock and buried her hands in Serena's thick winter fur. Daylight was more than half gone.

From the trees, Jynx chuffed twice, loudly. The enforcers looked around uneasily.

Serena's ears pricked forward. Bethnee chuckled. "Yes, she definitely taunted you. Go play."

The dignified dire wolf unexpectedly turned and licked Bethnee's face, then bounded off into the woods after the snow leopard.

She stuck her hands in her coat pockets and dropped her head to stretch her neck for a moment. She listened to breezy gusts stirring branches, and drifted for a bit, pretending the sun was warm. In her first few months on the planet, any weather at all had disconcerted her, after years living in controlled space environments. Now the wind through the trees sounded like freedom.

The door to her cabin opened, and Cherkogin strode out. Axur and Kivo emerged a moment later, but angled toward Bethnee instead of following the commander. Cherkogin turned to look at Axur, then gave Bethnee a respectful nod. "We're clearing out. Thank you for your help, homesteaders. And congratulations, by the way." She turned and made an upward spiral motion to her enforcers, and walked down the path with them following.

Axur stood, fists on his hips, watching them go. Kivo sidled up to her and put his head on her knees. When the last, low thrum of high-low flitters finally faded, Axur held out a hand to her. "Could we go inside now? My dangly bits are getting cold."

She smiled and took his hand, and let him help pull her up. "Can't have that. You might need them."

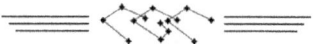

THE FRONT CABIN was finally warm again. She didn't want to go back to the cave until Axur's comms band monitoring confirmed that the enforcers had rounded up all the mercs and were on their way south.

She poured boiling water into the teapot. Axur sat at the kitchen-area counter she'd built to be comfortable for her height. Even though his face still sported streaks of dirt, and mud caked his long hair and beard, he was still plasma hot. She probably looked and smelled like something her weasel had dragged in. Felt like it, too.

Axur idly folded a thin towel into various shapes while they waited for the tea to steep. "I keep meaning to read the settlement contract, but legalese puts me to sleep. Tell me about this 'plus one' clause."

"It's complicated. Paying settlers can sponsor as many people as they like, and it confers homesteader rights to those people after a year, as long as they live on the settler's property. Those people can't do the same unless they wait another a year and buy or build their own homestead. Nonpaying but landed homesteaders like me can sponsor one person at a time."

Axur smiled. "Thank you." He gave her a speculative look. "What's Pranteaux's friction with you? Is it because you're a minder? 'Cause if that's the case, it's bullshit."

"No, he's a minder, too, a general filer who remembers everything. Nuñez says he's a control freak who overcompensates with his need for respect." She shrugged one shoulder. "I just think he's an asshole. Probably didn't help that I told him so to his face."

Axur laughed. She was going to miss the sound of it.

She poured tea into both the waiting cups. "Congratulations on the new job, by the way. Will you have to move to the spaceport?" She pushed one cup and a sugar stick across the counter toward him.

"I didn't take it." He dipped the stick into the tea and stirred once.

"Why?" Maybe he felt like he owed her. "This is just your legal residence for the year. You don't have to actually live here. You could be with Jumpers again, and it'd be a good use of your abilities. You like people. You liked Cherkogin." She pointed to his hanging poncho. "You're free."

"All valid points, and I'd have said yes if they'd offered when I first landed." He stroked Kivo's broad head, which was resting on his thigh. "But everything changed when I discovered the pets." He looked around at her tiny cabin. "I never had my own home before. Being a planetary enforcer would take me away from home a lot." He swirled the sugar stick in his tea. "I liked being a Jumper.

They help people in trouble, and look after their own. But I volunteered for the medic training and kept up my language skills because they're often more effective than guns." He gave her a lopsided smile. "Don't tell any Jumpers I said that."

"Your secret's safe with me." She couldn't hold her answering smile for long. "You have a lot of assets. You could move to a bigger city and be a medic and rent your printer."

He stilled. "Do you want me to go?"

"No, I want you to stay, because I think I'm in love with you." She wrapped her arms around her ribs. "But it's not about me. I want what's right for you."

A slow smile stole across his face. "All the cities are in the south, and Serena would be miserable in the heat." He stood and eased his way around the end of the counter. "I know you'd take her, but Trouble wouldn't have anyone to watch over, so I'd have to leave him and the others with you, too. Kivo's a theft magnet, like Jynx, so I'd have to leave him, as well." He edged toward her, close enough to touch her. "And that means everyone I love would be here."

She looked up at his strong, kind face. "You could have anyone you want. Someone who can promise not to be scared with you. Someone who's normal."

"Normal is boring." He touched the scarred side of his neck with his cybernetic hand. "I'm no prize." She hadn't seen that vulnerable look on his face before.

"Because you're a cyborg?" She reached out to slip her hand into his. She stroked a thumb over the exposed biometal knuckle. "Cybernetics are a part of you, but they're not you. The man I know is caring, smart... beautiful." Her eyes welled with tears. "Anyone would be lucky to have you."

"What if the only one I want is a nova-hot veterinarian who loves animals?" He slid his other hand up her arm slowly and rested it on her shoulder.

Bethnee smiled. "Nuñez would be happy to hear it." She put a hand on Axur's waist. "She and her wife think you're sexy. They like to share a handsome man on special occasions."

Axur shook his head. "The only woman I want also has a cybernetic leopard and a hot-spring pool." He put his other hand on the side of her face, and wove his fingers into her hair.

She leaned into his touch. "As it so happens, the only man I want is tall and strong, and loves animals."

He lowered his head to hers, stopping just before their lips touched. "Do you still want to kiss me?"

She raised her hand to his face to caress his cheek. "More than anything. Do you want to be kissed?"

"More than anything." He met her halfway to join his lips with hers.

He tasted cool and sweet. Heat pooled in her abdomen and warmed her core. She pulled herself closer, wanting to share the heat with him. He left her mouth and trailed kisses to the side of her face. She gasped in a mix of pleasure and pain as he brushed by her sore jaw.

He pulled back to look at her face. "Sorry, I didn't think." He touched delicate fingers to her cheek. "I've just wanted you for so long. I love you."

She gave up fighting the tears and let them fall. "I love

you, too, but I'm a mess. Could we maybe talk about this in my geothermal pool?"

He gave her a lascivious grin. "*Naked* in your geothermal pool?"

She chuckled. "Yeah, naked." She boldly slid a hand around to cup his muscular ass. "I'm worried about your cold dangly bits."

15

They didn't make it to the pool as fast as Axur had hoped.

Security systems needed arming after he'd moved his runabout down to her landing pad and brought all his gear into her marvelous cave. Animals variously needed calling in, drying off, reassuring, feeding and watering, and cleaning up after. He and Bethnee needed food, too. Using his enhanced speed and strength burned through calories like dry kindling, and he didn't have Jumper nutrient rebalancer concentrates to compensate. Bethnee had pushed her talent limit to the edge, too.

Finally, she led him to the geothermal pool. She turned and kissed him. "Hello, new homesteader."

"Hey, yourself." He could drown in the depths of her eyes. "Can we get naked now?"

She laughed. "Yes." She started to pull her tunic up with trembling hands, but he stopped her. "I want to make love with you more than my next breath, but I don't want to scare you. We don't have to do this now." He slid a hand up to her shoulder. "I'm not a telepath or an empath, I'm just a flux-to-the-max Jumper. You have to tell me what's too much, or too fast, or too close."

"I'll try. Sometimes, it takes me by surprise, and I just have to ride it out." She held up shaking fingers. "This isn't from fear, it's from wanting you." She flattened her palm on his chest. "I haven't had a lover since I was seventeen, and that was sex in the back of prepaid autocabs. You'll have to tell me what's going on with you, too. I love your strength, but I can't read you. I tank at communicating with humans."

"As it happens, I have built-in capacity for comms." She snorted in amusement. He captured her fingers and kissed them. "We'll figure it out together."

They explored each other in the warm pool. He loved finding the places where he could make her gasp and moan, and helping her find the spots on him that sent fire through his every synapse. He carried her naked to her bed, and only had to evict four furry occupants before joining with her to give them both the pleasure they'd been seeking. Their bodies seemed to fit together, like they'd been made for each other.

When he awoke and turned the lights up a bit, he discovered the bed had been invaded by three cats, a ferwinkle, a foo dog, and a six-legged chimera. He had a feeling their bed would never be cold or empty.

Bethnee stirred and rolled to the side, eliciting a muffled meow of protest from Delta the cat. Bethnee sighed and rolled back to drape herself on Axur. He loved the feel of her skin on his, the scent of her, the weight of her on him.

"What time is it?" she asked.

He checked his chrono implant. "A little after zero one hundred."

She slid her hand up to caress his jaw with her thumb. "Can't sleep in a strange bed?" She tweaked his earlobe. "Or with a strange woman?"

"You're not strange, you're unconventional." She made a rude sound, and he laughed. "Cyborgs love unconventional women who live in caves." He wrapped his arm around her waist.

"Good," she said. "I love cyborgs who have their own freighters. And printers. And autodocs. And runabouts." She kissed him between each item she listed.

He laughed. "It's too far for my potential patients and customers, though. I like your idea of looking at the abandoned house next to Nuñez's to see if we can make it into a medical clinic." He kissed her hairline. "According to a forecaster friend of Cherkogin's, trouble is brewing in the Concordance, and frontier planets should expect an influx of refugees. Something to do with Ayorinn's Legacy. You know, those nonsensical poems that predict a radical vector change for civilization." He shook his head. "The CPS dismisses them as a hoax, but I don't trust the CPS much anymore."

She sat up slowly and stretched. "I'm going to the fresher and check on Trouble. Want some water?"

"Yes, please."

He watched her because he could, enjoying the sleek curve and sway of her slender hips as she walked. She hardly limped at all. As soon as he could afford it, he planned to take her on a trip south for full repairs and healing. He sat up and rearranged pillows, blankets, and animals so she'd have a place to sit when she came back.

She returned carrying a glass of water and the wrapped Solstice Day present he'd given her. Trouble the dog walked in behind her, less energetic than usual, but looking alert. She handed him the water, then helped Trouble up onto the bed next to Kivo.

She kneeled on the bed and stroked Trouble's head. "I'm not sorry Kanaway died."

"Me, either." Axur took a deep, steadying breath to keep the anger at bay. He wanted to resurrect the sick twist, just so he could kill him himself, more slowly.

She crawled toward him to sit next to him against the pillows, holding the present. "Can I open this now?"

"Sure." He watched her face as she unwrapped and opened the box.

After a moment, recognition dawned. She stroked the heart-shaped piece of fur and looked up at him with a smile. "You printed this?"

"Yes." He loved her quick mind. "I've been working on a formula for synthskin patches for me, so I thought I'd experiment with synthfur for Jynx's leg. She deserves to be free to go outside whenever she wants."

She put the fur back in the box and put it on the nearby ledge, then kissed his shoulder. "It's a perfect gift."

She slid herself under his arm. "I've been thinking. Even if nothing comes of the forecaster's prediction, it wouldn't hurt to plan for an influx of new people, anyway. Once word gets around you're a trained medic with an autodoc and willing to take trade, more people will visit Tanimai, and some will stay."

"I guess I'm the first of the influx, then." He picked up her hand and kissed her fingers. "Lucky for me, I fell madly in love with a woman with a homestead and built-in pet family."

"We're the lucky ones." She kissed his chest. "I think you should talk to Cherkogin again. Offer to be on reserve, train with them monthly. You'd learn things you can't find out from just listening to their comms. Then we could prepare better, if we do get more refugees."

"You wouldn't mind?" His two potentially serious relationships while in the military had foundered when their assignments had taken one or both of them away for ten-days at a time. "I have to admit I was tempted, but you're more important to me."

"I appreciate that, but you've got skills you should be using." With a somewhat awkward move, she straddled his thighs and faced him. "Strength. Comms. Languages. Making friends. Blowing things up." She rested her hands on his shoulders and gave him a crafty smile. "Make them pay you in hard credit."

He laughed. "Now the truth comes out."

"Yep," she said. "We have to finish more of the cave so your animals can be comfortable when we're here." They'd decided to spend time at both her place and his, to maintain his homestead claim. "That takes renting the rock laser, and that takes hard credit."

He glided his hands up to her waist and leaned forward to give her a long, sensual kiss, with a promise of more. "I love a nova-hot woman who knows how to make a good trade."

ABOUT THE BOOK

Thanks for reading *Pet Trade*, and I hope you enjoyed meeting Axur, Bethnee, and their amazing pets. If you want more space opera, adventure, and romance, check out OVERLOAD FLUX. Two misfits have secrets they must keep. But if they expose the secrets of a corrupt pharma corp, they may end up dead.

Pet Trade originally appeared in the *Embrace the Romance: Pets in Space 2* anthology. Profits from the Pets in Space® anthologies support Hero-Dogs.org, a charity that provides trained support dogs to disabled U.S. veterans and first-responders to improve their quality of life. Their mission inspired my story. I figured if one pet was good, a dozen or more would be even better.

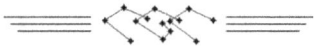

When the cure for a deadly disease is stolen, two misfits are all that stands between greed and intergalactic tragedy.

Luka Foxe can't let anyone know about his secret mental abilities. Debilitated by their influence when faced with violence, the brilliant forensic investigator now only takes assignments involving theft. But when he has to hunt down a hijacked vaccine for a galaxy-wide pandemic, the tragic first clue is his best friend's brutal murder.

Nightshift guard Mairwen Morganthur knows she must keep a low profile. The product of illegal genetic alteration, she's a lethal weapon with no social graces. But when she's tasked to protect a detective with frightening intuition, she finds herself falling for him even though he could expose her.

Racing to recover the cure for a galaxy-wide pandemic, Luka is surprised by his developing feelings for the capable-but-mysterious guard. And Mairwen may have to risk everything by revealing her identity, with deadly mercenaries hot on their tail.

Can the unlikely pair survive an interplanetary conspiracy long enough to save lives and find love?

Overload Flux is the first novel in the sweeping Central Galactic Concordance space opera series. If you like haunted characters, compelling mysteries, and interstellar romance, then you'll enjoy Carol Van Natta's epic tale.

Buy Overload Flux to uncover cosmic corruption today!

Author.CarolVanNatta.com/OF

*

ABOUT THE AUTHOR

Carol Van Natta is a USA TODAY bestselling science fiction and fantasy author. Works include the award-winning Central Galactic Concordance space opera series and the Ice Age Shifters® paranormal romance series. In addition, she edits the Pets in Space science fiction romance anthology.

She shares her Colorado home with just the right number of eccentric cats. Connect with her on the web at Author.CarolVanNatta.com.

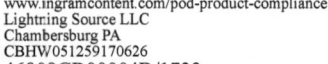